# G R JORDAN

# Corpse Reviver

*A Contessa Munroe Mystery #1*

This book was professionally typeset on Reedsy.
Find out more at reedsy.com

"Why fit in when you were born to stand out?"

Dr Seuss

# Contents


*Foreword* — iii
*Acknowledgement* — iv
*Novels by G R Jordan* — v
Chapter 1 — 1
Chapter 2 — 11
Chapter 3 — 20
Chapter 4 — 31
Chapter 5 — 41
Chapter 6 — 50
Chapter 7 — 60
Chapter 8 — 70
Chapter 9 — 79
Chapter 10 — 87
Chapter 11 — 96
Chapter 12 — 105
Chapter 13 — 113
Chapter 14 — 122
Chapter 15 — 129
Chapter 16 — 138
Chapter 17 — 147
Chapter 18 — 156
Chapter 19 — 166
Chapter 20 — 176
Chapter 21 — 184
Chapter 22 — 194

Chapter 23     204
*Read on to discover the Patrick Smythe series!*     210
*About the Author*     213
*Also by G R Jordan*     215

# Foreword

This story is set in the northern waters off Alaska and on a small cruise ship. Any persons named are entirely fictional, as is the vessel and the occurences onboard. But I do wish some of these people were real. And yes, I'd love to go cruising in those waters.

# Acknowledgement

To Susan, Jean and Rosemary for your work in bringing this novel to completion, your time and effort is deeply appreciated.

# Novels by G R Jordan

The Highlands and Islands Detective series (Crime)

1. Water's Edge
2. The Bothy
3. The Horror Weekend
4. The Small Ferry
5. Dead at Third Man
6. The Pirate Club
7. A Personal Agenda
8. A Just Punishment
9. The Numerous Deaths of Santa Claus
10. Our Gated Community
11. The Satchel
12. Culwich Alpha

The Contessa Munroe Mysteries (Cozy Mystery)

1. Corpse Reviver
2. Frostbite

The Patrick Smythe Series (Crime)

1. The Disappearance of Russell Hadleigh
2. The Graves of Calgary Bay

3.  The Fairy Pools Gathering

Austerley & Kirkgordon Series (Fantasy)

1.  Crescendo!
2.  The Darkness at Dillingham
3.  Dagon's Revenge
4.  Ship of Doom

Supernatural and Elder Threat Assessment Agency (SETAA) Series (Fantasy)

1.  Scarlett O'Meara: Beastmaster

Island Adventures Series (Cosy Fantasy Adventure)

1.  Surface Tensions

Dark Wen Series (Horror Fantasy)

1.  The Blasphemous Welcome
2.  The Demon's Chalice

# Chapter 1

Catriona ran her fingers through the ends of her curly hair, looking down at the ice disappearing beneath the helicopter. It was not her first helicopter ride, but this was such an exposed area. Everywhere was just ice—cold and clear. On one side, she could see the sea and she knew somewhere there would be a yacht waiting. To most people, this would have been a dream holiday, a chance to get away. But to the Contessa, this was a time to realign her life. Luigi was in the ground three weeks, and she was still coming to terms with losing the husband she barely knew. The infighting at the funeral amongst the family had disgusted her, and she did not have the heart to fight. Catriona had grabbed her chance when Luigi's brother had offered her the chance to take an annual stipend in return for leaving Italy. As much as she had loved Luigi in the brief time they had known each other, she did not want to keep close to his family.

These thoughts ran through her head as she sat, hand upon her chin, staring at the desolate waste below. Somewhere out there, there was life. A life that they were going to see, whatever existed this far north. She knew they were in the Arctic, but she was not sure where. Not that the woman beside her would know.

Tiffany had her earphones in; she always had those bloody things in, her long straight hair masking them. Catriona could see the wires coming out and running into the mobile in her pocket. For God's sake, they were whizzing their way across some of the greatest views on Earth. She, Catriona, had a reason to be sad, a reason to be down. But Tiff . . .they had never brought her Tiff just looked bored.

Tiffany Munroe was Catriona's niece. Most people would miss this as Tiffany was eighteen years old and Catriona was twenty-five. Being the youngest of the family on her side, Catriona was used to the idea that she had nephews and nieces close to her age. But Tiff was like Catriona in that she was the runt of the family. Yes, she had an excuse. Catriona had run off, taking a chance when an Italian had swept her off her feet—much to the disgust of her father and the rest of the family.

'You're destroying the clan,' he said. 'You need to marry well to lift us up in society.'

Honestly, thought Catriona, Scottish Society, as if that is happening anymore. We don't even spell our name correctly. Contessa Catriona Cullodena Munroe. She was not the typical aristocratic Scottish woman. It was not her fault; they had never brought her up to it. Her father was an imposter because they were not the proper Munros. Somewhere along the line, the family had left, gone to America, then come back. Her father, who had been born in America, did not seem to grasp this. Catriona, born in Scotland, was only too well-aware.

Tiff, or Tiffany Munroe, was her brother's daughter. But Tiffany was the last one of four. When she was growing up, everyone had said she was not right. Well, then she was like Catriona. Cat smiled at her, but Tiffany remained impassive, listening to her music, staring nowhere.

Looking out of the window, Cat saw a vessel in the distance. Its sleek outline made it look like the most expensive motor cruiser she had ever seen. Surely, there was a swimming pool on top or some sort of jacuzzi. She fancied that idea in this weather. Luigi would have fancied it. That is why he liked her. The two of them, they were very much pleasure seekers. What was the point of having wealth and money if you didn't use it? And during her few years with him, they had burnt a hole in the family's coffers. When Luigi had proposed, the family had gone crazy. But he had been good to his word. They had gone through with it, and Catriona was installed as the Contessa of Los Palermo. But three weeks after being married, she stood on the ski slopes, the Italian mountains, and held her husband's hand for the last time. Some sort of heart defect, they said. He just dropped right before her. At first, she thought he was playing around. But when he did not get back up, she realized her life was about to change again.

The helicopter flew in low beside the ship before rearing up and then setting itself gently down on the aft of the upper deck. From the window, Cat saw a man running forward to open the door. He was dressed impeccably in a ship's uniform, his hair neatly combed to one side, and he sported one of those half beards; not fully bushy, but more than just stubble.

The door opened, and a hand extended to her. Unbuckling her belt, Catriona let the man help her out of the aircraft and shepherd her off the deck towards the hallway. After depositing her just inside the door, the man smiled and then returned, ready to assist Tiffany off as well. But Tiff was out of the helicopter already, earphones still in, looking off the side of the boat. Cat shouted at her, but Tiffany heard nothing, and it took the young man to bring her niece back to her.

The man then ran to the helicopter and picked up their luggage, bringing it across before turning and waving at the helicopter. It lifted into the air and disappeared as the sound of its engines died away. Cat was escorted inside by the good-looking man who had first lifted her off the aircraft.

'You're most welcome, Contessa. My name is First Officer Jones, and I will give you a quick tour before you to get ready for your first excursion with us. On behalf of Mr Hughes, may I welcome you on board his yacht, the Cream Top.'

Catriona extended her hand, shaking the man's firm grip. She was not immune to the figure he cut. The only thing he missed from his white shirt and black trousers was a white hat, presumably not worn because of the helicopter and the risk of the hat disappearing into the sea. There were gold epaulets on his shoulder, which impressed Catriona, although she did not know what they represented. *First officer, he had said.*

'If I may escort you to the bridge where you can meet the captain.'

Catriona nodded and was ready to follow the young man. But he held out his arm, and she interlinked hers, allowing herself to be promenaded to the bridge.

Being introduced as Contessa was nice, thought Catriona, even though she had barely got used to it. The family did not call her by it. They saw her as an outsider coming in, and she had no title really as a Munroe. Her father liked to think he was a landowner, but he had bought in and did not have a Baronial title. Not that it bothered Catriona at all, and Tiff certainly did not regard her as a Contessa.

Catriona had understood Tiff as someone who really did not fit in either. Autistic was what they said about Tiff, but that term said only so much and you really did not know what the person was like. In some ways, Tiff was an extremely easy companion. She said nothing. She did not bother you unless she wanted something. And generally, she did not care if you talked to her or not. During her time of grief, Catriona appreciated this, whereas everyone else wanted to pitch in and share their grief with you. All Cat had wanted to do was get away, ignore the family, and just have some time on her own thinking about Luigi. And Tiffany provided this, sat in some corner somewhere else, earphones in, occasionally turning up to ask when lunch was, but otherwise, keeping well out of the way.

Most people thought they were sisters because of the closeness in age. But there was something in Catriona that felt for Tiff. The family had rejected her, much as they had Cat. When Luigi died, the family had only talked of money, saying that Cat could have a large stipend if she just got the hell out of Italy. Cat thought Tiff could benefit from this money and asked if she wanted to join Cat in seeing the world. The first question of 'Why would she?' seemed a little strange, but once it had been explained then Catriona was determined to go and enjoy life, Tiff thought it was worthwhile coming along too. In fact, Catriona had actually asked Tiff where was the first place she would like to go, and she had said one of those proper cruises up near the ice floes. Anyone having seen her arrive, and seeing Tiff with no expression on her face looking at the surrounding scenery, would never have guessed that she was the one responsible for the pair coming here.

'Welcome aboard, Contessa, and also to you. I take it this is your lady-in-waiting.'

The comment came from the captain, a woman with long

brunette hair. It was tied back in a simple ponytail. She wore a white blouse with epaulets on the shoulder covered in more gold than First Officer Jones, and she looked impressive despite her lack of height. Beside her was a younger woman again with tied-up, long hair, and who was darker in skin.

'I am afraid this will be only a quick welcome. I am Captain Jollye, and I will accompany you and First Officer Jones when we go onto the ice in approximately thirty minutes time. So, my apologies for rushing you, Contessa, but if you can be ready, we'll be departing on one of the boats for the ice floes over there. I am sure you will discover the other guests throughout the day. And my employer, Mr Hughes, regrets his absence at the moment, but he is just preparing for the trip as well. He says he will welcome you onboard properly this evening.'

Five minutes later, Catriona stood in one of the plushest suites on a boat she had ever seen. The bedsheets were silky to touch and the wardrobe space was fantastic. Even the bathroom, while compact, had one of those showers you can indulge yourself in, standing there and letting the water hit you from all angles. She was doing this, aware of the time. She needed to be ready within the next fifteen minutes.

Cat pondered about what to wear to something like this from her broad selection of clothes. There were some smart dresses, striking for dinner and that, but she would not run around on ice floes in those. Surely, all you needed were simple jeans and jumpers. Not that she could not look the part in either of them.

Stepping from the shower, she took a towel and dried herself down before turning and admiring herself in the mirror. What was it about someone passing on, but you suddenly wondered, did you look different from before? Luigi had always been one to tell her how good she looked. When she got down and feared that she was not something, Luigi was ready to tell her she was. Now, she needed to do it for herself.

But the low self-esteem she held herself in was part of her problem and the reason she jumped around at parties, where she made an arse of herself. Sometimes she just drank all those cocktails and let herself go. There were too many incidents. Too many times when she was, well, caught in compromising positions, that was probably the best way to put it. But life was going on and she had to get on with it.

Wrapping the towel around her, she stepped back into the cabin and saw Tiffany sitting on the bed, still dressed in the clothes she had arrived in.

'Tiff, come on. We're off to the ice floe. Fifteen minutes, you need to be ready.'

Tiff turned round and stared at her. 'I'm not going. What do I want to go to an ice floe for?'

'You were the one that wanted to come here. You specifically said that you wanted to see animals and all these other things here. I don't know what's here. You do, and you wanted to see them. Come on. Get changed.'

'But I do not want to go,' said Tiff. 'You cannot make me go.'

'I cannot make you go,' said Cat. 'But you're bloody well going. Come on, get your arse into gear.'

'I am ready anyway. I don't need to wear anything different.'

Cat looked at what her niece was wearing. Surely, she needs to change the trainer for some boots, some warmer trousers or jeans, and a coat. And there was nothing on her head. This was what bothered Cat about Tiff. You could not actually argue with her. You could not tell Tiff to do this or do that because automatically she would refuse and do the opposite, even if it was in her worst interests. This helped Cat because Tiff would stand up to the family in a way Cat could only envy. But other times, it was a pain in the arse.

'Fine, you just leave it then. Thank God. But I'm going to see some polar bears.'

'Are you sure there are polar bears here?' said Tiff. 'I didn't think they were present here.'

'Well, you would know. So, come on and point at what is here, Tiff.' And with that Cat turned her back and opened the wardrobe. She saw the fleece-lined trousers that she had purchased back in Italy. They were comfortable, yet tight. But she felt like she wanted a baggy jumper over the top.

Cat liked to dress cute, and she liked to look the part. But she was no tart, and the cream jumper she put on top was classy. She finished it with a cream bobble hat and her ski sunglasses. Looking at herself in the mirror, she decided she look dignified enough for someone who was so recently widowed, but classy enough to hold the name of Contessa. Yes, it was frivolous. But what did she have now, other than the frivolity?

Turning around, she saw Tiff putting on some boots and a black bobble hat. Tiff's clothes were a style all of her own. Subdued, but definitely coordinated. Not that Tiffany made any fuss about what she wore. She just wore it and people admired her for it.

'Come on, time to get on the boat.'

The Contessa was almost the last person onto the boat, most of the party having gone ahead. She climbed on board, ably assisted by First Officer Jones, who gave her a smile that she could not read, Cat sat down beside an older woman who promptly shook her hand.

'Hello, I am Sarah Gosling.'

Taking the woman's hand, Cat said, 'Catriona.' And watched the woman's face drop.

'You're the Contessa, aren't you? That's amazing. I've never met royalty before.'

'I am not royalty, Sarah. And it is just Catriona. There is no need for formality here.' Cat looked at the woman's clothing, and while a lot of them seemed to be a poor fit, they all looked incredibly new. She also looked a little uncomfortable in them, as if not used to wearing this quality of clothing.

'What do you do, Sarah?' Catriona asks politely, noticing that Tiff was ignoring the woman completely.

'I actually used to be a cleaner in a school,' she said. 'But now, having won the lottery, I have decided to try to live a life that I couldn't have before. I get to meet people like you.'

Catriona could not understand why this would be important to anyone, but she smiled at the woman, and then looked out towards the ice pack the boat was now heading for. 'Have you ever seen anything like this before?' she asked.

'Nothing at all,' answered Sara Gosling.

'Me neither,' said Catriona. 'But I am looking forward to it. Tiff here is an expert on a lot of these things. She is an expert in most things, to be honest. Walking encyclopaedia. Isn't that right, Tiff?' Catriona smiled over at her niece. But the earphones were in and Tiff heard nothing, sitting with an expressionless face.

'Is she all right?' asked Sarah, concerned.

It was a great way to say things, but it seemed to get the message across every time. 'She is in her own place, so I can't tell.'

'Oh, right,' said Sarah. Smiling, but clearly not really understanding much at all. 'That might be challenging.'

'You have no idea,' said Catriona. The women sat in smiling silence. Then Catriona looked at the rear of the small vessel they were in, and First Officer Jones. He kept smiling at her. She wondered if he was just being good with the punters, or was there something else there. He seemed to smile at her a lot. In fairness, he had quite the figure. Broad shoulders, certainly in good shape. But she couldn't tell what he was really like underneath. Catriona was obviously trying to size the man up too much because Tiff tapped her on the shoulder, explaining they had arrived at the ice floe. She caught a quick smile from First Officer Jones. Clearly, he knew she was looking at him before he ran over and helped her off the boat onto the ice floe. It was a precarious movement, and he had to assist her by wrapping his arm around her twice. *Caring anyway*, she thought. *Although, I am a punter.*

'Over this way,' said Tiff. 'Come on. Stop messing with the boat. I want to have a look at this.'

That was Tiff all over. Not going on the trip, not doing this, and then suddenly I am doing this. I want to go here; you have to follow. Sometimes, Catriona could not keep up but left the first officer behind, giving him a dainty little smile before she did so. She followed Sarah Gosling across the ice. The three women were making towards another group of people less than two hundred yards away, and there was some excitement, including within Catriona. She had never been somewhere like this, and she wondered what they would look at. Calmly she walked forward, following Tiff's footsteps. And then a single gunshot rang out.

# Chapter 2

Sarah Gosling shrieked beside Catriona, causing Cat to jump. But ahead of her, Tiff was running forward. Cat was caught in two minds for a moment, not knowing whether to turn and look after Sarah, or go with her niece who had run. She wondered just what Tiff would get up to on arrival.

As Cat took off towards the sound of the gunshot, she was overtaken by the first officer, bolting hard across the ice. As Tiff approached the large group ahead, Cat could see Captain Jollye standing, decked in winter gear, but waving her hands and ushering everyone backwards.

'Can you all remain here? Hold everyone here. Jones, take charge while I see to what's happened. Keep everyone back until we know what has occurred.' The first officer did as instructed, and as Captain Jollye turned away, Cat saw Tiff try to squeeze past to follow her. First Officer Jones put out a firm hand and ushered the young woman back.

'I am afraid that is not somewhere you want to go. Let the Captain deal with this.'

'Who's dying there?' said a voice. Cat spotted an older grey-haired man, and then saw Sarah rushing towards him. She put her arm around him, but he seemed to dismiss her, and asked again, 'What's happened? Who was it?'

A younger man stepping forward, maybe in his late twenties, with curly brown hair on top, said, 'Is there anything I can do? I've seen this sort of thing in my line of work. I'm a first aider, maybe I can assist.' Again, a hand was put up, and First Officer Jones explained to everyone to stay back. Beyond him, Catriona could see at least three people. There was the Captain, the man who had helped carry their bags when they came off the helicopter, and the younger woman who had been on the bridge.

'If you can just let the Captain get on with it,' said the first officer. 'The Captain, Mr Denny, and Miss Limpet are all qualified first-aiders. If something has happened to Mr Hughes, they will deal with it.'

Cat looked around her, and it was a scene of confusion. She was amongst people she didn't know, but a young woman, possibly around her own age with short black hair, stepped forward and the first officer let her run past.

'Who's that?' asked Cat. The first officer smiled back, 'That's Ms Forsythe. She is Mr Hughes's PA. I believe she's also got some first-aid training, so let's all just stay back.'

A broad-shouldered older man with a large white beard stepped forward to the first officer.

'Maybe I can help, I'm a Professor. Fragrance, come with me.'

Cat turned to see a blonde-haired woman around her own age. She seemed in shock and was not for following the bearded man. Meanwhile, an older woman with brown mousey hair that fell down onto her shoulders, was looking concerned.

'Why would he have that gun with him? What's he trying to

shoot out here?'

'Sometimes he likes to hunt—Mr Hughes. Well, let us hope nothing untoward has happened,' said the first officer.

'There was blood! There was definitely blood! I could see blood. I wasn't that far from him.'

'Mr Kopeck, calm down, okay? Just calm down. Everyone, stay here until we know what's happening,' reiterated First officer Jones.

The commotion continued for a few minutes until Cat saw the Captain returning to the first officer. She whispered something in his ear, at which he turned and walked off towards where the incident happened, while the Captain stood with everyone. She raised her arms, calling for quiet, before addressing the gathering.

'I'm sorry to say that there's been a tragic accident,' said Captain Jollye. 'Your host, and my employer, has unfortunately died because of gunshot wounds. It appears that the weapon misfired, and I would ask that we all just stay calm.'

There were a few gasps, a few cries, and tears. One or two of the women then turned to others, sobbing on their shoulders. Tiff, however, was jumping at the bit to get past the Captain, and Cat could see her moving sideways to get a better look.

'What sort of gun was it? Was it a rifle or a handgun?'

Catriona nearly died on the spot. Marching over to Tiff, she took her by the arm. 'Not the time, Tiff, not the time. Come and stand here with everyone else.'

'But I really want to know what type of gun it was. How did it misfire? But did it really misfire? Did anyone see it?'

'I saw the blood come up,' said Mr Kopeck. 'There was definitely a lot of blood.'

'Did he shoot himself then? Was it through the head? Did it

hit some other part of his body or the heart? There was a lot of blood. That means he must have hit an artery,' said Tiff.

The Captain's face looked like thunder. 'If you do not mind, Contessa, if you could get hold of your lady. That sort of talk is not helpful at this point in time.'

'My apologies, Captain,' said Catriona, 'but she is different from the rest of us. She means nothing by it.'

'I'm different, and what?' said Tiff, hands now outstretched, looking as if Cat had wounded her.

'Fine, but deal with her please,' said the Captain. 'We have enough to get on with ourselves. I think the safest thing to happen is that we'll start taking everyone back to the boat, and I'd ask you to remain in your cabins until we come for you. This is purely precautionary and allows the rest of us to deal with this situation, and I will decide what we will do from there. I'll then have us all meet in the stateroom and discuss the options.'

'Are you sure you don't require any help?' asked the older woman with the mousey hair.

'No, but thank you, Mrs Bridge. It's much appreciated, but it's best if you all step away and allow me to deal with this.'

Mrs Bridge at this point decided that she was now in charge of the guests, and turning, started ushering everyone back to the boat, until a voice shouted after her, 'Don't get on board! Wait by the edge until we get some crew there with you, and we can get you back over.' Cat turned around and followed the rest of the group back towards the small boat, but Tiff kept looking back over her shoulder.

'How do you think he died? Kind of really went wrong or something else happened. Why would you come all the way out here just to get shot? That's crazy, isn't it?'

Catriona rolled her eyes at Tiff, 'Not now, not now! I've had a bit of experience what it's like when people are dead around you. Many people don't like that sort of talk, Tiff. Didn't go down well at the funeral at home, did it? I know you mean well, but they don't. Enough.'

It was a five-minute wait at the boat before First Officer Jones showed up and took the passengers back over to the main cruiser. When they arrived in their small groups, they were met on board by a bald-headed man who looked to be in the later stages of his career. The first officer introduced him as Ivan Popov, the chef. With the mention of his name, Tiff was gazing at him and Catriona could see that the man was staring back. His eyes were full of mistrust, and when she walked past him, Cat thought she could smell some sort of drink.

'Mr Popov, now that we're all aboard, I'll need to head back and help the Captain. Can you prepare some food, to be ready in the stateroom in about an hour, at which point we'll have all the guests remain there. If everyone would for now kindly go to your cabins, I will inform you with an update as soon as we have it. One hour in the stateroom please, everyone.'

Tiff was keen to stay up on the upper deck and look out across at the ice floe for as long as possible. It took Catriona dragging her by the arm to get her to come towards the guest cabins. From what Cat could see, there were several groups. Along with the white-bearded man who purported to be a professor, there was the younger woman with the blonde hair. And the colour of the man's beard made Cat think they may be father and daughter, or even father and granddaughter. Sarah Gosling and Mr Kopeck occupied the cabin close to Cat and Tiff. Quite what their relationship was, Cat did not know.

Then, she saw the man with the curly, brown hair enter a room on his own. As she tried to drag Tiff away from looking at the scene in the floe, Mrs Bridge came up to assist.

'Are you all right, love? I just thought I'd ask. Oh, sorry, I just called you love, didn't I? It's Contessa, isn't it? They said you were arriving, and Mr Hughes was quite chuffed about having royalty on board.'

Cat shook her head, 'I'm not royalty. My husband was a Count, Los Palermo, but I'm actually Scottish. And it's Catriona. Cat, if you wish.'

'Hi, I'm Harriet, Harriet Bridge. You've probably seen my fitness clubs and that.'

Catriona wanted to say yes and build the woman up, but Cat had been in Italy for the last few years and did not know what the woman was talking about. But the woman looked in good shape.

'I'm sorry, but I do not quite recognise the name. Do you do any of the classes and stuff yourself?'

'I'm actually online. That's how I got into the fitness clubs. I started off doing online workouts and built it up—probably the biggest in the country now. When I say the country, I mean the UK. That's how I made my millions.'

'Well, delighted to meet you,' said Cat. 'Unfortunately, I haven't been around, so I'm a bit behind on quite what's happening in the UK. What I do know is Tiff is still looking over there, and should be in our cabin. So, if you take one arm, I'll take the other. Let's see if we can walk her back.'

Tiff was not the most cooperative. It took three minutes of cajoling and then an outright lift of the arms to drag Tiff back into the cabin. After thanking Mrs Bridge at the door, Catriona turned with eyes of fire, throwing her bobble hat onto the chair by the bed.

'What do you think you're doing? They've just had somebody die. They need to get things sorted. We've been asked to just come in here and wait, and you are all over it. What are you doing?'

'It seems a bit weird, doesn't it? Somebody goes out hunting with a gun and dies? I just wanted to see what happened. So, it doesn't make you suspicious?' asked Tiff.

'No, it doesn't,' said Catriona. 'It doesn't. What it does do, is it pisses me off, for this is an inauspicious start to a holiday when I am trying to get away from it. And when people die, this is the thing. People want to be left alone. That's his crew out there. They probably knew him well. They're probably upset, and the captain's got to sit there and look after everyone else and make sure things are done properly. And you, Tiff, march into that as if you have a right to nose anywhere. Well, enough. That's not how we behave. Anyway, we've got an hour to sit on our bum and then we can go downstairs and hear what's happening. We could be on a helicopter back out of here quickly.'

'Well, that won't bother me,' said Tiff. 'I didn't want to come here anyway.'

Catriona nearly swung for her. But she took a deep breath and undid her coat and fleece-lined trousers. 'Well, I think the key thing is we carry ourselves with a bit more dignity than we just have. Although I have to say, if they have got any cocktails tonight, I'm on them. Might as well enjoy myself before we go anywhere. Either that or we find a hotel on land where I could put my feet up by the pool and just forget about what happened.'

'But you didn't even know him,' said Tiff.

'I wasn't talking about that. I'm talking about Luigi.'

'Oh, Luigi,' said Tiff. There was no sign of care. There was no sign of any love from her. But then, that was what Catriona expected from Tiff. Everything in life was about Tiff, and you had to understand that. All the focus was on Tiff. If it was happening outside Tiff's world, it didn't happen, it did not exist. It had taken Catriona a long while to realise that this was not Tiff being uncaring because when she decided to care, she cared in abundance. It's just it all had to come inside her world before that even became possible.

Catriona sat down, took out a hairbrush, and started brushing. After two minutes, she stopped. It was what she did when something was bothering her. She turned around to Tiff, who was lying on the bed, earphones in.

'Oy, why are you worried about it? Why are you concerned?'

'Just seems strange to me,' said Tiff, taking out her earphones, 'the fact he just blew himself away. Unusual. How many guns do that? I hear many people accidentally shooting someone else, not themselves. Something's not right. Trust me. Something's not right.'

Catriona turned back to the mirror in front of her and began brushing her hair again. It was one thing she had going for her. Whatever she did with her hair, it always looked good, but it's best was to just hang naturally. It rippled out at the end, dangling down past her neck, and set off what figure she had. She'd always been brought up by her mother to look good. After all, someday, she'd have to bag herself a husband. Cat had always been told that, and her mother believed Cat would never have a career. Not because she shouldn't, but because she couldn't.

Unlike Tiff, Cat was not the cleverest. At least not the most academic. She liked to think she was clever in other ways, but nobody ever seemed to back her up on that. Well, she was clever enough to bag the man who now, even though he was gone, was still looking after her. The last time she checked the bank balance, she couldn't believe what she saw. She could do this all year and still not be broke, and every year more money was going in. In some ways, she landed on her feet. In reality, she'd lost everything. What was the point of going through all this high life with no one to share it with?

But maybe she'd get back into the game as they put it. It was a game, wasn't it? All pretending to look like this and that. Fortunately, when Luigi found the real Cat underneath, he liked her so much that he'd asked her to marry him. Why the hell did he have to die?

Cat looked around and saw the fridge, sitting under the dressing table, opened it up, and saw the miniature bottles underneath. She took two shots of Tequila, put them in a glass, and downed them. Her mother would have despaired, but then again, she wasn't here. What the hell's the use anyway when he died?

Pulling herself together, Cat dug inside her bag for a book. She had started it some time ago and had got halfway through it. She began to read, but none of the words were going in. Instead, she lifted her eyes and looked at Tiff on the bed. Tiff always seemed happy within herself, even if her face never showed a smile. *Maybe I could get to that stage in life. Maybe I could be certainly happy within myself.* Cat looked toward the fridge with the miniatures again. *Until then, maybe these will have to be my friends.*

# Chapter 3

Catriona made sure she was down in the stateroom precisely one hour later. Tiff and herself were one of the first there, along with Mrs Bridge. On the arrival of the professor, everyone remained silent as they looked around for the crew. Presently, the young man who collected the bags of Catriona and Tiff from the helicopter arrived.

'My name is Denny, and I'm a deckhand on board. They have asked me to come down and get you some drinks while you wait for the captain. Is there anything I can get for you?' Catriona did not wish to look forward, but with everything going on, she was feeling very unbalanced.

'Gin and Tonic,' she said. 'Maybe something stronger a little bit later.'

'That is an excellent choice!' said Mrs Bridge. 'By all means, Mr Denny, pour us a few of those. Will you join us, professor?'

The man nodded, stroking his impressive white beard. 'It is all a shame, isn't it?' he said. 'Everything just feels a little flat. I was hoping to see plenty of the animals today, but with this sort of thing going on we will not be doing much more.' Mr Kopeck interrupted them along with Sarah Gosling, arm-in-arm, but he seemed uncomfortable. Looking at Cat as he walked into the room, Kopeck made for Catriona, and as Denny went to hand her drink to her, Kopeck took it from him, instead offering it to Cat himself.

'I thank you,' said Catriona, 'but maybe you should look to get Sarah one as well, Mr Kopeck.'

'Call me Tyrrell,' he said. 'You probably recognise me.'

Catriona shook her head, looking a little embarrassed. 'In exactly what field should I be looking for you?'

The man looked somewhat disturbed. 'I'm in the movies,' he said. 'I know it has been a while since the last big Hollywood one. I got my first big break in the year 2000 on the *Turn of the Century*. I'm sure you would have remembered it.'

'I doubt it. I think you misunderstand my age, Tyrrell. I'm twenty-five, would have been a five-year-old. So, unless you were in—I don't know—something about munchkins, I doubt that I would have seen it.'

Tyrrell Kopeck turned away, looking down at his shoes until he found Mr Denny and ordered a large scotch and something for Sarah Gosling. Catriona felt bad because Tiff burst out laughing at the comment. This was Catriona's curse. She did not mean to be nasty, but things just occurred to her and she felt she had to say them. She really needed to learn to keep her mouth in check. Sarah Gosling was coming forward, and she looked like she was on the warpath.

'I think that was harsh. Tyrrell's struggling with his self-esteem; the least you could do would be to be a bit kinder.'

*Interesting*, thought Catriona, *because he had that look when he saw me. That look you don't get from a man who is accompanying a woman he wants to be with. But maybe this is a bad time to bring that up, even if it would make Tiffany laugh.*

'I apologise. Sometimes I say things I don't mean.'

'But he deserved every bit of it,' said Mrs Bridge. 'Don't you pay any heed? His eyes have been everywhere on this trip.'

'How long have you been here?' asked Catriona, as Mrs Gosling fumed.

'We have been on the go a week,' said Mrs Bridge. 'Call me Harriet. No need for any of these formal names?'

'And I am Cat, always Cat. Some people get very confused about the Contessa. I have been mistaken for royalty twice.'

'Well, you certainly do not strike me as royalty?'

'Not anymore,' said Sarah Gosling.  and turned away to comfort her partner.

'Don't pay any attention to them!' said Harriet. 'She's only got him because of her money. He's not interested in her at all. He's already made passes at me. I think I have got a bit more class than some washed-up movie-star.'

'Yes, but I don't like to offend,' said Catriona. 'And as for you,' she said, turning to Tiffany, 'you can keep that mouth shut next time. Do not laugh in the poor man's face just because I said something daft.'

Tiffany turned and looked at Catriona. 'What? What did I do? You said it.' And with that, Tiffany grabbed a gin and tonic and marched off to the side of the room, suddenly engrossed in the pictures on the wall.

The stateroom had a wooden floor and walls while a large table occupied the side of the room. Catriona realised they brought this out for dining as she saw a fixing on the floor where a table could be attached. Maybe they moved it to one side to accommodate everyone standing together. The room was filling up now, and she saw the younger woman who had run off to Mr Hughes on the ice flow. 'Who's that?' asked Catriona.

'That,' said Harriet, 'is Mr Hughes's PA, although many

people think she's more than a PA, too.'

'That's rough, isn't it?'

'Really?' said Harriet. 'I don't bring my PA on these trips and trust me, he's a lovely young man of twenty-five, but I'm not after that from him. Maybe it's the men. Take the professor there.'

'The professor?' said Catriona. 'You mean the one with his daughter? Or is it his granddaughter?'

'That is not his daughter or his granddaughter,' said Harriet. 'That is his partner. Wait for this . . . Fragrance Paradise. Did you ever hear the like of it? Who on earth calls themselves Fragrance Paradise? She sounds like something off a menu or drinks card at that. Still, here comes Mr Fogherty.'

The pair turned to see the man with the curly hair enter the room. Making a straight line for Contessa, he almost bowed and Cat felt herself blushing red.

'It's fine. I'm not royalty; a simple handshake will do.' With that, she extended her hand.

'Mr Fogherty,' the man mumbled. 'Also known as Jack and forgive me for not saying hello earlier. Just been having trouble with my leg.'

'What's up with it?' asked Catriona, suddenly aware that Tiffany was leaning over her shoulder.

'He took the corner wrong, spun off, crashed, wrecked his leg, and he's now building it back up again.'

'Apologies, Mr Fogherty. This is my niece, Tiffany. She's quite forward. I wouldn't take anything she says too directly if you understand me.'

The man nodded. 'Well, she is correct. The racing car spun out from me and I ended up in a crash. My fault, stupid, but there you go. Out for the season, so I'm here recovering. It's difficult getting away from it all, from people. I don't know if you understand that.'

'Oh, I do understand that,' said Catriona, 'and you're most welcome. If you're looking to get away from it all, you can join me.'

The man smiled and then turned around, waving down Mr Denny for a drink. 'Would you like another one?'

'Don't mind if I do,' said Catriona. 'Harriet?' Soon another round of drinks arrived and Catriona was suddenly struggling to remember that a man had just died.

There seemed to be a buzz in the room that was brought to an abrupt halt when someone clapped their hands. When everyone parted, it surprised Cat to see the compact figure of Captain Jollye. The woman really was a powerhouse, although she was only five foot three. But with her hair hanging down behind her and her white immaculate blouse and crisp black trousers, she cut an imposing figure.

'Thank you, everyone. My apologies for not getting back to you quicker. Mr Hughes, or rather the body of Mr Hughes, is now lying in his cabin and will remain there behind a locked door, until we make port. We are some distance from the nearest port, which was quite deliberate as you know, as we should be on another three weeks of travel. I have contacted the authorities about the accident who are quite happy for an officer to come aboard when we make land. However, in the meantime, we see no reason why we should curtail our trip. As close as we were to Mr Hughes, I do believe it's what he would have expected as well. And so, I intend to take you ladies and gentlemen round the rest of this glorious part of the world. Unless anyone desperately needs to go home, in which case we shall call for the helicopter to arrive. Would anyone like to partake of that offer?'

The room went silent and Captain Jollye scanned everyone, making sure that she would miss no one. 'With that in mind, I think we should have dinner as normal. And so, I'll see you all back here in two hours' time. I remind you all—especially our newcomers—that dinner is formal. And I believe tonight our Chef Mr Popov will deliver an impressive fish course. I'm sure we all look forward to that. In the absence of Mr Hughes, I shall take place at the Captain's table and you are all most welcome. Eight o'clock sharp, please, ladies and gentlemen. Now, if you'll forgive me, I need to make sure we get back on our way, so we arrive at our next stop on time. If any of you have concerns about what we are doing or are suffering from what happened today, please do come and see me, as First Officer Jones is more than just a simple first aider and has had paramedic training.

'However, we shall not be dull and we shall not be mournful. Mr Hughes would have wanted us to enjoy the surrounding land on this vessel. So, we shall. And I shall see you all for cocktails at eight.' With that, Captain Jollye turned on her heel, walking smartly out of the room.

Catriona was somewhat surprised, but having had a couple of gin and tonics, she was more than happy to continue the voyage. She wanted to stay away from people, and here things seemed good. Things were quiet, except for the dead man, of course, but, as they had stored him aboard and safely out of reach, there was no need to waste this time.

Catriona accepted another gin and tonic from Mr Denny. She heard someone coughing behind her. Turning around, she stared up into the eyes of First Officer Jones.

'Contessa,' he said, 'may I ask for your company tonight at

the Captain's table? As first officer, I have a place near the top and I'd be delighted if you would occupy my guest seat.'

Catriona was taken aback. She found the man intriguing. He was certainly well built, and part of her felt desperate enough to take a chance. But she looked over and saw Tiff once again, glaring up at photographs on the walls of the stateroom.

'Please don't take this the wrong way,' said Catriona, 'but I really should be with Tiff. Tiffany is not what we would call a normal person.' Almost immediately, Catriona felt bad. 'Well, actually she is normal, but she's different, differently normal. Yes, she's simply different and I think having someone beside her is a good idea.'

First officer Scott nodded. 'Well, I understand that, but she can actually sit on the other side of you. I can arrange that. I really insist that I take your arm tonight.'

*Well, this looks promising, Catriona.* 'I would be delighted in that case,' she said. 'Eight o'clock for cocktails, I believe the captain said.'

'And I shall show you my dab hand at making them,' said Mr Jones.

'Until then, Contessa, if you forgive me, I have duties to perform.'

Catriona said, 'If you are going to take my arm, you're going to call me Catriona. I will not accept Contessa. I've come over here to get away from being a Contessa.'

'And in that case,' said Mr Jones, 'you can call me Scott. I shall see you at eight.'

As the first officer walked away, Catriona became aware that Mrs Bridge was staring straight at her. 'You work fast, love, don't you? Well, I can't blame you. Certainly, a man of physique, and if he's got the brain to match, you might have to be careful. I'll be shoving you out of the way.'

The woman turned away laughing, and Catriona saw Tiff looking across the room at her. Then a few seconds later, Tiff came over.

'What does he want? He was talking a lot to you.'

'Well, pardon me for speaking to people.'

'No, he was speaking to you. What did he want?'

'Well,' said Catriona, blushing slightly. 'He's asking me to dinner tonight, but he says you can come too and sit beside me.'

'That was fast, wasn't it? I think he's up to something. You should be careful. With the way you are at the moment, you'll fall for anyone.'

'I will not!' steamed Catriona. 'And would you kindly keep that sort of comment to yourself until we're in a room. Actually, in fact, keep it to yourself. I don't need to be babysat by you. Can I remind you who's the aunt and who's the niece here?'

'You're twenty-five; get over the big mother act. Anyway, they have cocktails tonight I heard; that will be you gone.'

'Enough!' said Catriona. 'Can we try to act a bit classier?'

Tiff shrugged her shoulders and disappeared off to look at the pictures again.

An hour later, Catriona was back up in her room. Tiffany was still downstairs examining pictures and walking around the boat, but Catriona decided she needed to make an effort tonight. She didn't see why she shouldn't enjoy herself and decided she needed another shower and to get ready. Stepping inside, she felt the water hit her skin, relishing the heat. She heard Tiffany come in through the door. Sometimes, she wished Tiffany weren't there. She had not been long with her and, certainly at the funeral, was a great help to have another black sheep of the family. Tiff was quite caring then. Maybe the enormity of the situation had got through to her.

Everyone else was talking about how her husband's brother had to take up the running of the family. Catriona felt left out. She was a widow at the end of the day. His mother was still alive. Yes, and God knows the woman hated Catriona from the day she set eyes on her. But was everyone ignorant of what Catriona was going through? Her own family had not come over for the funeral, besides her brother and Tiffany. Tiffany was probably kicked out as much as anything as they saw a chance to get rid of her for a couple of days. Catriona's brother, Mark, had not been unkind, but he really hadn't wanted to be there. He had been dead set against Catriona's marriage, although he had attended, unlike her parents.

Mark was very uptight, but he was a wonderful brother, and she loved him dearly. She knew he would never let her just go, unlike her parents and aunt. Even when she first met Luigi and disappeared on weekends, Mark always kept in touch while their parents were giving her the cold shoulder. Yes, Mark was there, the perfect pet of her parents. But he also was her brother, and she missed him terribly.

It was at his insistence that she took Mark's daughter, Tiffany, on board with her. Cat knew he would be sad at home without her, but Tiffany was never truly welcomed. Now she was having a life with Cat that she never could have had elsewhere. Mark was also the only person who got to call her by her middle name, Cullodena. Who the hell ever heard of a name like that? Father must have been drunk when he thought of it. But in fairness, although she never used it, but Mark teased her with it. He was allowed to.

With all the soap rinsed off her shoulders, Catriona then stepped out of the shower. Rubbing herself down with the towel, she grabbed a brush, stood in front of the long mirror, looking at herself as she brushed her hair. Like most people, she was slightly disappointed with how she looked, so she stopped, turned around, and came out of the shower room to dress.

Luigi always said she dressed best when at her simplest. So, she put on a long flowing black dress with thin straps over the shoulders. It was classy and yet had a sassy touch to it. From her jewellery box, she took out the chain with a cross, a wedding gift from Luigi. She never quite clocked how the Italians' mix with faith had actually worked. Even his mother had faith, despite being blessed with such a barbed tongue. But the cross had been important to him, and she only wished she'd had longer to understand why.

'What do you think?' said Catriona, turning around and standing in front of Tiffany.

'Definitely cleared up; you on the pull?'

'I'm sorry? On the pull. Where did you hear that? I am dressing for dinner and you need to do as well.'

'Why do we have to dress for dinner? What's wrong with these jeans? They cost enough.'

'Come on, time to get up,' said Catriona, hauling her up off the bed.

'I'm not wearing a dress. You know that. Besides, somebody's dead. Why are we acting like this?'

'Acting like what?'

'Acting like this, as if nothing's happened. The man is dead; surely we should look at why.'

'It was a shooting accident. The captain said so,' said

Catriona, shaking her head.

'And you trust her,' said Tiffany. 'I don't buy it. I don't buy it—guns going off killing someone. You kill someone else with a gun. You don't kill yourself. It didn't backfire.'

'They didn't say that.'

'And where's the weapon? I'd like to see the weapon.'

'Shut up!' said Catriona. 'I am going downstairs dressed like this because there is a rather good-looking man who I'm going to enjoy the company of this evening. You're going to come down and you're going to smile with feeling. And you will say nothing to interrupt or come out with something daft.'

'What, you mean like you did to that film guy. That was classic.'

'That was rude! And you're not going to do that.'

'No! I'll wait for you to do that,' laughed Tiffany. 'I'll put on trousers and a blouse, but that's it. I am not going in a dress.'

Catriona nodded, 'Okay. Then let's get downstairs and find out what's happening.'

'I think something's happening,' said Tiffany. 'Don't get too pissed tonight. You're simple enough as it is; you'll never understand what's happening if you're drunk.'

# Chapter 4

Catriona was feeling good when she walked down the small stairs to the stateroom at the centre of the ship. Although there was a set of double doors, they were quite narrow, and she swept into the room with Tiffany in her wake. Tiff had taken a while to get ready, and Catriona was desperately rushing her on as she wished to meet the first officer. He had seemed so enamoured with her before. She had made no decisions about him, but she was up for a little bit of fun, and certainly, Cat felt a lot looser than when she arrived. Probably it was the gin and tonic talking, but she felt good about tonight.

The room was full of rather elegant-looking people. Harriet Bridge, complete with her glasses, stood in an elegant ball gown. Catriona felt it was over the top. Maybe that was not how an older woman saw it. Beside her was Miss Forsythe, the PA of Ernest Hughes, dressed in a classy black cocktail dress. Alongside stood the professor, his white beard eminent and set off against his black dinner jacket. On his arm was Fragrance Paradise, her blonde hair running down onto bare shoulders. Looking at her, Catriona felt she was overdressed, as Fragrance seemed to display as much flesh as possible.

Across the room, Sarah Gosling wore a smart black number.

Beside her, in a white formal jacket, Tyrrell Kopeck seemed to be gazing at everybody except Sarah. Jack Fogherty looked out of place in his dinner jacket. Maybe he was a man who was more comfortable behind the wheel of a car. The crew were dressed in uniform except for the captain.

Catriona marvelled at how elegant the woman looked. She had a fake fur around her shoulders, but the smart dress she wore was certainly alluring to many of the men in the room. In some ways, Cat was jealous of her, able to go from the professional-looking woman to the classy but sexy woman in the space of an hour. Despite being small, Captain Jollye held the room.

As Catriona swept in, she felt her arm being taken and looked up to see the smiling face of her bearded escort. First Officer Scott Jones was still in his uniform, but now he wore a smart dress jacket over the top. He spun Cat on his arm towards the cocktail bar. This was a small trolley that had been erected at the side, and as he moved behind it, Scott Jones smiled, announcing he was doing a special tonight.

'Corpse Reviver, maybe a little tasteless but I thought it was the one that we should go for.'

'Where'd you learn to make cocktails?' asked Catriona, watching the man operate the shaker and the glasses with a dab hand.

'Oh, I've done many jobs before, making my way onto boats doing something like this. The more skills you have, the easier you are to employ. Here, try this,' said Jones, handing over a fizzing glass.

Catriona took a sip, and then she took another. 'Wow, that's got quite a kick to it,' she said. 'Have you got one for Tiff as well?'

Looking over her shoulder, Catriona realised that Tiffany was no longer there, but was standing beside Jack Fogherty, the young racing car driver. It was quite normal to see Tiffany in a room not talking to anyone. What was unusual was how she was standing there and listening as the injured racing car driver seemed to be explaining the basics of going around some circuit. Tiff was even nodding as if she was appreciating what he was saying. Cat doubted this, but she didn't care. Tiff was away and enjoying herself, and she was going to delight in having First Officer Jones on her arm.

The evening proceeded much as Cat wanted, and when they sat down to dinner, they were treated to an amazing display of shellfish, all caught in the local waters. Despite not being hungry, Cat managed to polish off everything that came to her plate, and by the time that she stood up at the end, she was feeling quite tipsy. There were numerous bottles of wine on the table, and Scott Jones excused himself as he and the rest of the crew moved the table to one side.

Music filled the room. Jones then stepped across with his hand out to Catriona, asking if he could have this dance. At first in the early part of the evening, the tunes were jazzy, and Cat felt tired as if her feet were forced to traipse back and forward across the floor. Catriona was no dancer, but clearly Jones was. Catriona's biggest surprise, however, was Tiffany dancing with Fogherty.

It was a cordial atmosphere in the room, until the chef, Mr Popov, was brought up. During the round of applause for the food he provided, the man belched, and it was clear to Cat that he had been drinking. Discreetly, Captain Jollye manoeuvred him out of the way, and more music was played.

As the clock proceeded past midnight, the music became

slower and Catriona found herself dancing cheek to cheek in the arms of Mr Jones. An hour later, having consumed several brandies, Cat let Jones walk her to her cabin, and she could tell that the man wanted to come inside.

'Maybe not tonight, Scott,' she said. 'It's only been a short while since Luigi passed on, and I'm not quite sure I'm ready for that side yet. Maybe in a while.' She reached up and gave him a peck on the cheek. She felt a hand come up to her neck and pull her closer, and suddenly she was kissing properly. A few seconds later, they broke off.

'Good night,' said the first officer before waiting to see her inside the door.

Closing the door behind her, Catriona lent her back against it, thinking over the time she'd had. She flicked the light switch on, expecting to see Tiff in bed, ready to tell her about the evening, but Tiff was not there. *Well, wherever she is, I hope Tiff's enjoying herself.* With that, Cat collapsed onto the bed.

Catriona wasn't sure if she'd switched the light out, but it was certainly on when she woke up. There was screaming from outside. She instantly leapt out of the bed. Tiffany was not about and Cat's first thought was that she was upsetting someone, but then she thought the screaming was too manic, too crazy, and threw open the door, stepping out into the main corridor of the guest cabins. At the far end of the corridor, where the doors led out onto the deck, Cat saw Sarah Gosling screaming. She was still dressed, dolled up in the same outfit she had been wearing in the Stateroom, but her face was white as a sheet. Cat ran towards her and saw Tiffany coming from the deck side along with Jack Fogherty.

'Sarah, what's wrong?' shouted Cat. 'Are you okay? Where's Tyrrell? Is he not with you?'

'Tyrrell went to bed, but I've seen him. I've seen him.'

'You've seen Tyrrell? Where?' asked Cat.

'No. Mr Hughes. I've seen Ernest. Ernest walked along here.'

Catriona stopped in her tracks. The woman looked so drunk, but she was clearly white as a sheet. Maybe she thought she had seen him; maybe the drink was playing tricks with her mind.

'Where did you see him?' asked Tiff, arriving abruptly behind the woman, Jack Fogherty on her shoulder. 'He came along here. Up, he went up towards the cabin, up towards the owner's cabin along the corridor, down to the end. He came out of my cabin.'

'He can't have done that,' said Cat. 'He's dead. He's lying up there.'

'I tell you,' screamed the woman, 'he's not dead. He came along here.'

Cat heard footsteps behind her, and suddenly First Officer Scott Jones was on her shoulder. She felt two hands grab her by the waist and the man appeared from behind saying, 'Is everything all right?'

'It's okay, Scott. Sarah's just had a fright. She thought she saw your boss.'

'But he's dead. He's up in his cabin. That's where we laid him out. He's there.'

'Are you sure?' said Tiff, 'Was he definitely dead?'

'Stop it,' said Catriona. 'I don't need that right now, Tiff.'

'But it's a reasonable question. Sarah says she saw him.'

Catriona turned around to Scott, putting hands on his shoulder and whispering in his ear. 'I'm sorry, she's on the spectrum. This is what Tiff's going to ask. Just humour her as best you can without upsetting Sarah.'

'He was in my cabin. He came from my cabin,' said Sarah.

'Well, let's take a look inside,' said Scott, 'Come on.' His hands lifted off Catriona and took Sarah by the shoulders, walking her towards her cabin. 'I'll just open it for you,' he said. Pulling the door back, Cat could see the light was on.

'We switched that off before we left. Ask Tyrrell. Tyrrell will tell you the light wasn't on.'

'Maybe somebody else should go in,' said Tiff, 'Come on, Jack—we should step inside first.' Jack looked like he didn't want to, but Tiff grabbed him by the arm, dragging him in front of Jones and Sarah. 'Mr Tyrrell? Mr Tyrrell, are you there?' shouted Tiffany. 'There's a load of us coming in. We don't want to disturb you in case you're sleeping. Are you there?' There was no sound, and Cat watched Tiff walk into the room. Cat thought she would be nervous doing something like this, as there was possibly something up, and clearly, Jack Fogherty felt that way. Cat could see his hand shake, but Tiff was fine. She stepped in matter-of-factly, looked around, then turned around, saying, 'It's empty. You've made a right mess like, but, other than that, it's fine.'

Scott Jones led Sarah Gosling into the room and as soon as she saw it, she began to shriek again. 'Who the hell did this? What did he do? He's been through my stuff.' Cat couldn't help herself but follow them in, and sure enough, the room was in a mess. Doors have been opened, things have been overturned, and Sarah Gosling now sat down on the bed and began to cry.

'Well, somebody's been in here,' said Tiff. 'Who's to say it wasn't the owner?'

Catriona rolled her eyes at Tiff. This would not help. If something was going on, the last thing we needed was ghost stories in the middle of it.

'Can we all just exit, please, and I shall deal with this.' Looking over her shoulder, Cat saw Captain Jollye still in her evening dress, but she bustled into the room like she owned the place. 'I'll need to talk to Mrs Gosling,' said the captain. 'And ask if everyone else would leave.'

'That's a good idea,' said Tiff. 'Maybe your first officer could show us your boss. Sarah says he was in this room and then walked back up to his own room. I think we need to make sure he's dead.'

The Captain raised her eyebrows and Catriona thought Tiffany was going to get a barrage of abuse, but instead, Jollye turned to the first officer. 'Mr Jones, can you escort everyone from the room? And just for clarity, can you take someone to confirm that Mr Hughes is still lying at peace in his own cabin? I suggest you take the Contessa. I think everyone can rely on her word.'

Catriona nearly died. Why her title meant that she was a good fit as a witness, she had no idea. But she needed to go along with this because, otherwise, Tiff was going to start off. As Catriona turned for the door, she nearly bumped into Fragrance Paradise, who had the professor behind her. 'What's happened?' asked the man.

'Out, everyone,' said Captain Jollye, 'Everyone out; grab your coats and go stand on the main deck. I shall come and speak to you momentarily. Mrs Gosling has had a shock. Has anyone located Mr Kopeck? Can someone please locate Mr Kopeck?' Catriona stepped out of the room and leaned up against the hallway. She looked at where the owner's cabin was, towards the front of the ship.

'I'll be with you in a minute,' said Scott. 'Just let me get everybody else out onto the deck.'

'Make sure Tiff goes right there; otherwise, she'll follow us like anything,' said Catriona, 'The last thing we need is her playing around with a body.' Scott smiled and nodded, and Catriona was left standing, looking down the corridor. As much as she didn't want to believe in dead people getting up and walking around, this was clearly disturbing that someone was in a cabin and looking for something. *Had they been disturbed? Made a run for it?* She was unsure. But then she saw the young PA of the owner heading towards her from the owner's cabin.

'What's going on?' she asked.

'There's been a bit of a commotion in Mrs Gosling's room, I'm afraid. You might go and see the captain; she might need your help.' Meanwhile, Harriet Bridge could be heard outside getting rather annoyed that somebody's room had been turned over. Again, calls were put out for Tyrrell Kopeck. Cat could see Mr Denny outside, as well as Chef Ivan Popov. Then Tara Limpet swung past her, coming from the cabin owner's suite.

'Captain, I'm here. What can I do for you?'

Once again, Captain Jollye was stunningly impressive. She had all the guests outside being calmed down, while she took personal care of Sarah Gosling. Scott Jones returned to Catriona, and led her down the hallway, towards the owner's cabin. He took out a key, opened it, and then flicked on the light switch.

The room was breath taking. A large bed in the far corner, with silk sheets, but with a rather strange black bag on top of it. There was plenty of gold around, an ostentatious show, and the room was filled with all sorts of devices. Glancing through to the bathroom, Cat saw there was even a small tub, possibly a jacuzzi.

'It is quite something, isn't it?' said Scott, 'I'm afraid we don't have time to look around. I need you to come over and make sure that Mr Hughes is where he should be.' Catriona nodded and walked over to the body bag. Almost matter-of-factly, Scott pulled the zip, and then slid it to reveal a face in front of Cat. It looked pale, with short-cropped hair and quite a rounded face. The man seemed to be in the prime of life except for his colour. And Cat, maybe emboldened by the amount of alcohol she had drunk that night, quietly stood and stared at him. She stretched out for the side of his neck, looking for a pulse. Before she could reach, Scott grabbed her hand. 'Just in case there's any investigation, you don't want to be getting your fingerprints on him.'

'Good idea—sorry,' said Catriona.

'It's my first body, but as you can see, he's quite dead,' said Scott.

'Indeed,' said Catriona. 'Let's get out of here. I could do with a sleep.' As she turned to walk across the room, she felt a hand on her shoulder. Scott spun around and pulled her close.

'I wish I could treat you to a cabin like this,' he said. And with that, he grabbed her, roughly kissing her.

Catriona pushed back, falling off the man. 'Sorry. I've had too much to drink. You need to be sure to say these things when I'm standing properly.'

It was a faint, a play, because she knew where the man was going. Cat wasn't ready for that sort of thing yet, but neither did she want to stand in this room much longer, with a body sitting on a bed. It took another ten minutes before everyone was tucked safely away back inside their cabins, and Cat noted that Tiff locked the door, then moved a chair behind it.

'What are you doing?' said Cat, trying to haul herself out of her dress.

'We can't be too careful if we've got dead men walking around.'

'Dead men don't walk, Tiff. You know that. And he was dead. Trust me, I saw him.'

'Did you check for a pulse? Was he completely dead? Did you check if he was breathing?'

'He didn't look like he was breathing to me, and he was inside a bag. He was white.'

Tiff shook her head. 'You know nothing about bodies, do you? No point letting you check for anything.'

Catriona let her dress drop, pulling some pyjamas out of her suitcase. 'I am going to bed. Enough talk about dead bodies and people walking around, okay? I've had a rather nice night, and now I just want to sleep.' Cat lay down on her bed and then turned over. 'And what about you tonight? You had a nice night, didn't you?'

'I found out a lot about Mr Fogherty,' said Tiff. 'He's quite dull, really. He talked all about engines to me, even mapped out the Monte Carlo car circuit. I think he's driving it wrong.'

Catriona laid back on the bed, then her head hit the pillow. Her hair splayed out behind her. The girl was impossible. She looked over, and Tiff was sitting on the chair facing the door. 'Stay up if you want to,' said Catriona, 'but for God's sake, turn out the light.'

# Chapter 5

'**A**re you going to lie there all day?' said Catriona, looking at her niece. Tiff was sprawled out on the bed, wrapped up in a set of pyjamas with a duvet thrown over her, her long straight black hair above the sheets.

'I, uh . . . um, whatever!'

'Well, I'm going to go and get breakfast. Don't be lying around all day.' With that, Catriona put on a fleece jacket and made her way out from the guest quarters downstairs to the stateroom where last night she had danced with the first officer. Everything had seemed to be going well until the screams in the middle of the night and the break-in at Sarah Gosling's room.

The woman had seemed so scared, and she thought she'd seen a ghost. But, at the end of the day, Catriona had gone in and looked at the man's dead body. In truth, Cat had not much experience with dead bodies. She'd seen Luigi's, and it was a face that would haunt her, the life gone from the love she had. But beyond that, Cat couldn't remember actually ever seeing one.

Had she examined it correctly? It didn't seem to be breathing, and the skin was white, pale. That was correct, wasn't it? After somebody had died, the blood would leave them, made them pale. In truth, Cat had no idea, but regardless, she was going down for breakfast and going to get on with this cruise.

As she entered the stateroom, she realised that there was no one else there. However, on the side, a number of breakfast items had been left, as well as canteens with sausage and egg, and some flasks of coffee and tea. Sitting down at one of the tables, she had just a croissant as her stomach felt a little queasy. Cat was certainly tipsy last night, and her head, while not pounding, was not feeling a hundred percent. However, some black coffee, a little croissant, and she should be fine. The stateroom was so quiet; in fact, the whole ship was. When she'd arrived, everything had been a flutter. There had been all the excitement and panic around the death of Mr Hughes and then they carried on almost as if nothing had happened until Mr Hughes was spotted walking around.

Was there a sense of party? Well, in a way, yes. Presumably, not many people knew Mr Hughes. Certainly, Catriona didn't, but maybe they did. That was something she could look into. No, that was for Tiff. Tiff would do that. She was probably already asking more and more questions. Well, at least once she got up she would. And then she would wander around with her theories explaining to Cat that this was how this person did it. At the end of the day, Cat would have to calm her down, enjoy the couple of weeks, and then fly off to the next adventure.

She thought about skiing next, but it was cold. Luigi loved skiing. Cat didn't; she liked the warm fires and the brandies once she was inside. When she finished her breakfast, Cat realised that no one else was about, and looked out at the rear deck. In a corner, there was a jacuzzi bubbling over. She took a look around for a button before realising she could start it anytime she wanted with a foot sensor. Making her way back to her cabin, she then changed into a bikini, then her dressing gown around her, and after shouting at Tiff again to get up, made her way back to the jacuzzi. The air was cold as she walked out onto the deck, and she almost half ran until she reached the jacuzzi, throwing her gown on the floor and jumping into the bubbles. The water was warm and she lay back, eyes closed, enjoying the soothing action, working on the aching limbs from last night's dancing.

'Excuse me, ma'am, would you like something? Can I get you a drink or something else?'

Cat opened her eyes and saw the chef standing before her. He seemed to be swaying a little. She wondered if he'd been drinking. 'Actually, yes,' she said. 'What can you do?'

'I saw you last night and you enjoyed the cocktails. I make you a cocktail, yes?'

'Sounds good,' said Catriona. She paid enough for this cruise, she might as well enjoy the most of it. Lying back, she closed her eyes again, but after a few minutes, she opened them with a distinct feeling that someone was watching her. The chef was still stood there looking down at her. Catriona's instinct was to throw her arms around herself, but she was underwater and there were bubbles. He couldn't see anything. Possibly, that made it creepier. 'Yes?' said Catriona.

'I was wondering what type of cocktail you would want.'

'It's the morning. I love a Tom Collins, something with a bit of pep to get me going, don't you think?'

'As you wish.' And with that, the chef turned on his heel and walked away. Catriona closed her eyes again and laid back. A few minutes later, she got that feeling again, opening her eyes to see standing before her, Fragrance Paradise.

'Do you mind if I join you?' said the woman.

'Well, there's plenty of room,' said Catriona, 'Not at all.' Deep inside, however, she was quite annoyed. After all, she had this space all to herself. Maybe that was the answer. Don't go away on cruises—just buy yourself a big jacuzzi for the back of the house. No, she needed to go out and do things. Besides, an outdoor jacuzzi in Scotland didn't sound great. 'How are you?' asked Fragrance Paradise. 'It's all been a bit of a shock. Hasn't it?'

'Well, it's not what I'm used to,' said Catriona. 'Did you know Mr Hughes?'

'No, not really. The Professor does. He talked about him a lot. I think they go quite far back. Well, as far back as a man of Mr Hughes's age. He was quite delightful. He whisked me across the floor last week, certainly a bit of a dancer and worth so much money. I mean, Heinrich has got brains. That's partly why it attracts me to him. But Mr Hughes, he had the money.'

'So, you and Professor Heinrich, you're a couple? Is that correct?'

Fragrance looked down at the water before looking back up, 'Everyone says he's a bit old, and yes, he is. But, he has a heck of a mind. I can't compare with the mind he's got, and he disappears off for that intellectual challenge. He reads his books; he disappears at times. But, he told me he just wants female company. Yeah, it works for us, though I did like it when Mr Hughes took me across the floor. Heinrich's not the most romantic. Clever, very astute, but not the most romantic. What about you? Have you not got a man in your life?'

Catriona shifted uncomfortably in the jacuzzi. This was not a question she wanted. Life with Luigi was over. She didn't want to bring it up again. It had been good and she missed it, but invariably when she had to talk about it, it always ended up in talking about his family and how nice she was roaming, almost without a home.

'I'm a widow, Luigi died a month or two ago.'

'Oh, I'm so sorry,' said Fragrance. 'Was it something unnatural?'

*What a question?* thought Catriona. 'No, he just had a heart defect,' said Cat. 'Something they said they couldn't have picked up, died right in front of me. But he was fun, you know? Like you say about Mr Hughes, Luigi was fun; both of us were really black sheep of the family. He's clear of that now, God rest him. I'm still the black sheep.'

'But Contessa, what a title,' said Fragrance. 'I'd love to have that, be able to walk into any room and they ask you who you are, and your first words are Contessa. It's so classy.'

'And that's me, all class,' laughed Catriona. 'In truth, I'm Contessa in name. His family didn't really like me. My family doesn't like me that much either. None of them liked Tiff, maybe even less, which is why she is with me.'

'Is that your sister?' asked Fragrance.

'No, my niece,' said Catriona. 'But what about you? You say you're with Heinrich, but how?'

Fragrance started looking around her. 'Well, he was my Professor, and I dropped out of the university, but he came after me. I was no student. So clearly, he wanted something else. I could provide that. He excites me with his mind, and in truth, he's got a bit of money to take me places. This is what I like; this is what I want. Can you understand that?'

Catriona nodded and then saw the chef arriving.

'One Tom Collins for madam. Can I get you a drink?' The chef stood and stared at Fragrance. Again, he seemed to sway slightly.

'Yes. Do we have any champagne?' The chef nodded. 'Let's have some of that then. Bring a glass for my friend.'

Catriona took in a deep breath. *That sort of cruise, was it? She'd be lucky to remember any of it, the way this was going.* 'Tell me, Fragrance,' said Catriona as the chef departed, 'Does he look a little—?'

'Pissed?' said Fragrance, 'Sorry, such a vulgar word. Drunk as a skunk. Is that how the English say it?'

'English? So, you're not English? Because your accent is particularly good.'

'I'm the daughter of a German serviceman. I was brought up in England. But no, I'm German through and through, as is Heinrich. That's why I was back at university, sent there by my parents, sent to try to give me a sense of home after being away for all those years. But alas, all it did was teach me to drink, enjoy myself, and attach myself to a man who can provide me with what I need.'

'Well, sounds good to me,' said Catriona. 'Oh, who's this coming?' A man with greying hair was arriving in the tightest pair of swimming trunks Catriona had ever seen. She wasn't quite sure it suited him because the man was at least forty, and that stomach was not as toned as he thought it was. 'But hey, we don't judge people on figures these days, do we?' she said, and then realised what a lie that was.

'Mr Kopeck,' said Fragrance, 'Are you joining us today?'

'Absolutely,' he said. 'I assume there's room for one more?' Catriona looked at the size of the jacuzzi. You could have fitted six or seven in quite comfortably, so yes, there was room for one more. However, when Tyrrell jumped into the jacuzzi, he sat right between both women.

'Well, there's nothing like being nice and close together, is there?' said Catriona as the man lay back and let both arms sneak out behind them. The arm was less than half a foot from Catriona's shoulder and she swore if he touched her, she was moving.

'How's Mrs Gosling today? Is Sarah okay?' asked Catriona.

'What a palaver,' said Tyrrell. 'Honestly, seeing dead men walking about.'

'But your room, it was turned inside out,' said Fragrance. 'What were they looking for?'

'Well, I guess that would be the joy of being a millionaire.'

'How come,' said Catriona. 'I don't think anyone here is lacking money. Of course, that's assuming it was her stuff that was being looked at. You're sleeping in there as well, aren't you?'

The man nodded, but not with a happy face. 'How come you're here with her?' asked Catriona. 'Excuse me being so blunt, but you don't quite look like a normal pair.' The man's arm moved and touched Catriona's shoulder. She noted his other arm and hand around Fragrance's shoulder.

'Well, it's like this, ladies, when you get to my age, you just have to accept that stardom happens. She's paying me a lot of money to come with her on this trip. So yeah, I came.'

'Well, she probably wouldn't want to see you like this then,' said Catriona.

'Indeed not, but I doubt she'll be up before midday. She rarely rises. That's true, isn't it, Fragrance?' Catriona felt the man's hand on the back of her neck, and saw he was doing the same to Fragrance. Just then the chef arrived with the bottle of champagne and two glasses.

'I think Mr Kopeck will take one of those glasses. He's got a hand that needs something to occupy it.'

Tyrrell Kopeck looked shocked but removed his hand from Catriona's neck. She noted that Fragrance seemed unmoved by the man's action. And the chef then poured two glasses of champagne, and the three sat there in the jacuzzi drinking.

'So, is there a man in your life?' asked Tyrrell to Catriona. 'A Contessa, and a good-looking one like yourself. I fear I may be too late.'

'Yes, you're right,' said Catriona. 'I prefer much younger men. The grey coming through in your hair really doesn't work for me.'

Fragrance nearly spat her drink out, and Mr Kopeck rounded admirably, 'Sometimes, maturity has its benefits.'

'Maybe if you're a Rolls-Royce,' said Catriona. 'But to be honest, most cars, once they're past ten years old, aren't worth driving anymore.' And there was that tongue again, but this time she was happy to deliver it. In fact, part of Catriona wished Tiff were there because she would have laughed in the man's face. What a cheek sticking his hand on the back of her neck. She wasn't having any of that. But she was still aware that Fragrance was quite happy sitting there, almost enjoying the hand rubbing her neck.

'I think there are still excursions today?' said Tyrrell. 'I don't think Mrs Gosling is up for much. I might take an excursion myself, join you ladies.'

'We'll have to see if there's room. Maybe you could come along with Tiff. I think she'd be an interesting partner for you,' said Catriona. Again, she watched Fragrance laugh.

'Yes, your niece, somebody said. Is something wrong with her?'

Cat felt the rage building inside. Tiff was different. Tiff

could wind Catriona up in all sorts of ways. But Tiff was her niece. Tiff was family, and nobody spoke about Tiff as if there was something wrong with her, because there was nothing wrong with her. She was simply different. Catriona was fed up with people who were different, being called wrong.

'Tiff is a genius, and Tiff will get to the bottom of what's happening here. You wait and see.' *Now, where did that come from? thought Catriona. She'll get to the bottom of what? We've got a hysterical woman seeing dead men walking around; we've got an upturned room.*

'So, you think there's something up,' said Fragrance.

'Well, I'm not a hundred percent sure,' said Catriona, 'But Tiff is. She's very clever. She's quite different, Mr Kopeck, and she certainly wouldn't like to be handled. I wouldn't like to see her handled.' Tyrrell Kopeck leant away from Catriona as she said the words.

'Well, absolutely, very pleasant girl, very pleasant. But yes, yes, understand fully, needs her own space. Absolutely. But like I say, I could join you this afternoon. Are you going on the excursion?'

'Oh, yes, come,' said Fragrance. 'I think I could enjoy an excursion with you. Heinrich's having to do some study. So, please come and join me.' Catriona raised her glass. 'Absolutely. This sounds more and more like fun.'

# Chapter 6

Tiff finally raised herself at midday and struggled down to the stateroom for a light lunch with Catriona, who ushered her niece quickly back upstairs once they had eaten. Cat hurried Tiff into a change of clothes and then to the side of the boat, where they jumped into a small rib that took them to a glacier nearby.

Despite the protestations of Tyrrell Kopeck to join them, Captain Jollye had said there was only enough room in the rib for six people, and it was an all-female excursion.

And so it was Cat and Tiff joined Captain Jollye, Tara Limpet - the crew hand, Harriett Bridge, and Fragrance Paradise. The captain was dressed for the cold in her thermal trousers and large jacket, but she had let her hair down. Catriona thought her the most impressive woman..

Cat sat at the rear beside Fragrance, who seemed amused by Catriona's ramblings. Meanwhile, Tiff was pestering Mrs Bridge with questions.

'So how did you know Mister Ernest Hughes?' asked Tiff.

'Are you Miss Marple's daughter or something?' asked Mrs Bridge, laughing. 'Well, if you must know, he did want to take over my business. I told him I was not interested. Our business was business; we got on well. And we made some minor other investments together. He has been quite a friend since. Just a business friend, nothing personal. I have been invited to his cruise ship several times. I am sorry—sad to see him go. Ernest was fun to be around.'

'That is, if he is indeed gone,' said Tiff.

From the front of the boat, the captain turned around, her hair swinging behind her. 'We will have less of that talk. We took your sister to see him. He is dead, and he is not coming back, so kindly have a bit of respect.' With that, the captain turned back, looking out to the front of the boat as she approached the glacier.

'Well, all I am saying,' said Tiff, 'is that somebody was walking about. Somebody scared Mrs Gosling. So, somebody has to be doing that and we have also got an upturned room. What is all that about?'

Again, the captain turned around, her eyes now glaring at Tiff. 'Hey Contessa, would you kindly keep your fellow guest in order?' said the captain through gritted teeth. 'She is beginning to try my patience. Some of the crew were quite close to Mister Hughes. So, please, could we show some respect? We are doing our best to make this cruise as enjoyable as possible given what has happened.'

'And then if you look at the—'

Catriona leapt forward, grabbing Tiff, and pulling her down, placing a hand over her mouth. 'Shut up for once, shut up.' And then she whispered in her ear, 'If you are going to investigate something, do it more subtly. Just ask people who they are. Talk to them normally. Find out things. You are walking around like a bad Miss Marple.'

'It's not my fault. It is my first investigation,' said Tiff.

'All the same, be more subtle.' Tiff sat down and Catriona

could see that she was thinking deeply.

The thing about Tiff was that when she got the right idea in her head, she was devastating. But if the wrong idea was in her head or the wrong way to go about things was there, trying to change her approach was a nightmare.

Catriona decided she needed to make amends and slowly made her way up the rib until she was beside Captain Jollye. 'Captain,' said Catriona. 'I am sorry for my niece's behaviour. She is simply different.'

The captain nodded. 'We're all girls out here. Just us call me Louise, Contessa.'

'And I am Catriona.' She held her hand out to the captain and shook it. 'So, where are we and what are we likely to see?'

'We are hoping to see some seals just over the far side here. You may even see them feeding. It is quite amazing being close up to nature. If you are really lucky, you get to see some whales. But in truth, sometimes it is just nice to get away.'

'I don't like to speak ill of the guests in front of other guests, but Mister Kopeck has made approaches to me several times, so I am sick of him. Jack Fogherty is about as wooden as you can get, and the professor, frankly, is doing my head in, telling me how to run my boat. Sometimes a girl just needs a little space. I am sure you understand.'

Catriona did understand. Sometimes you just wanted to be on your own. And imagine being at sea all the time with the pressure on her. Captain Jollye was up against it. Catriona wondered what it would be like never to be able to just blow off a little steam. 'Do you ever get to be on the boat on your own?' she asked.

'Occasionally. Mister Hughes was more than just my employer. Several times a year he used to come away for his own personal holidays. A couple of times we went off without a crew. It is quite something running the boat with just the two of us.'

'The problem is when he comes away on business, Miss Forsythe tends to hang about and the girl does not want any competition if you understand me.'

Catriona nodded. 'He sounds like quite a man. I am sorry I missed him.' Catriona glanced at the side of the boat as she heard a splash. 'What was that?'

'That is one of your seals. Keep an eye out.' The captain shouted to the rear of the rib at Tara Limpet, 'Turn the rib around.' As they ran over the waves, Catriona saw the seals jumping in and out of the water.

'Tiff, look at that,' she shouted.

'Yeah, I can see it,' said Tiff.

Catriona forgot just how unexcited Tiff got about things. She almost preferred to read about them in a book than actually see them in real life. That was the difference between them. Catriona wanted life to be experienced. Tiff simply wanted to read about it and understand it.

The rib followed the seals for some ten minutes. Catriona enjoyed herself, placing her hand on the water as the rib ran along, Captain Jollye standing beside her, pointing here and there.

And for once, she felt she was getting to talk with someone on a level. Everyone else seemed impressed that she was a Contessa. But here she was talking to someone else at the top. Captain Jollye at the end of the day was in charge of the trip, and she was treating Cat almost like a sister.

'When we go onto the glacier, come and walk up front with me. Tara, do the tourist bit with the rest of them. But let us have some decent conversation,' said the captain.

When the rib came alongside the glacier and everyone had disembarked, Catriona watched Tiff and the rest following Tara around as she pointed out the wildlife in the sea. Captain Jollye called Catriona over and they headed off to the other side of the glacier.

'Oh, it is good to be away,' she said. 'I heard that you lost someone close as well.'

Catriona nodded. 'Yes, Luigi. Not that long ago. It is taking time, but . . .'

'It is going to be tough without Ernest,' said the captain. 'Yes, I did get to call him Earnest. He was a strange man though, never wanted to be tied down. But when he gave you his time, he gave you a hundred percent. I was one of the few to get an exceedingly small window into his life. I think I will miss that.'

Catriona stared at her face and eyes that looked sad. But something seemed missing. Cat had just experienced what losing a partner was like. It was the devastation of knowing they would not be back. Looking at the rest of your life wondering how that hole is going to be filled, no one to walk it with you now. But Captain Jollye looked like someone who was just having a temporary moment, like she was waiting for things to be restored. It was not a devastation, more like a temporary sadness.

'You learn to go on,' said Catriona. 'You have to. I mean, take Tiff, for instance. She is actually good company. For all the things that she is not, she keeps out of my way. And she makes me laugh. She is also able to laugh about things I say. That's important. I imagine you are very isolated being the captain.'

'More than you would know. But Earnest told me a lot about the people he spent his time with. And I am very aware that someone is doing something on this boat. Keep an eye out for me, Contessa. I could do with all the help I can get now that Earnest is gone.' With that, Captain Jollye embraced Catriona, placing her head on her shoulder.

The woman gripped Cat tightly, and she heard her begin to cry. Cat held her close. But again, there was something that just did not feel right about this. Something within Cat was screaming fraud, and she felt horrible for it. Maybe people just grieve differently. She is just a fantastically strong-looking woman who was having a moment on her shoulder. The least she could do was deliver some sisterly love.

From behind, Catriona heard a yell. Captain Jollye was straight up off her shoulder and looking over. Spinning around, Cat saw Tara Limpet running along the edge of the ice of the glacier.

'What is up, Miss Limpet?' shuddered Captain Jollye.

'I have lost one. I cannot find her. Miss Paradise is gone.'

Cat and the captain ran over towards the edge where Cat saw Tiff staring into the water.

'Did you see her, Tiff? Did you see her?' asked Catriona.

'No, she was behind us. I was talking to Miss Limpet, and she was behind us, and then.'

'Did you see her go in?', asked Cat.

'No, but she was there. Where has she gone?'

'Everyone, fan out around the glacier,' instructed Captain Jollye. 'Do not go close to the edge but search the water.' Cat ran back and forward looking in, Tiff accompanying her.

And then Tiff gave a cry. 'There! Right there!'

A hand was in the water. It was flailing desperately. Cat was watching, expecting a head to pop up at any minute, but then she saw the hand disappear back under the water. 'She is out there, captain! Only about twenty meters out,' cried Catriona. 'She has just gone under.'

'Get the boat, Limpet. Get the boat round.' Cat watched the two women run for the rib.

'She will not survive long in there,' said Tiff. 'It's cold. If she starts to sink, she is gone. We need to get her quick.'

Cat saw Harriett Bridge staring in disbelief; Fragrance, too.

By the time the captain got the rib round, the woman could be gone.

'Hold my jacket,' said Cat to Tiff.

'What are you doing? It is freezing in there. You'll perish.'

'Somebody has got to try. She's going down.' Cat pulled the jacket off, throwing it towards her niece. She then reached for her thermal trousers, pulling them down, kicking off her boots in the process. She was aware that she stood then in socks, her pants, and a t-shirt top. The cold raced across her thighs and legs and she gave a shudder.

'Don't be in there long. And quit looking back,' said Tiff. 'Otherwise, you will freeze and you'll go down, Cat!' she shuddered as Catriona dived off into the water.

Cat's face felt the cold first, and she knew in her heart that the last thing she needed to do was swim straight away. The cold ran through her body but she tried to think, remember what to do. *Slow down, float. Just float,* she thought. Slowly, gradually her head came back up to the surface, and there she was just bobbing around. Fortunately, the waves were not high and she was floating. Deciding she was able to move, Catriona began to swim towards where she had seen the hand.

Catriona had been brought up swimming and was well used to it. She had swum outdoor in sea conditions in Scotland and also in the lakes in Italy, after she had been married. With each stroke, she cut through the water, moving at a pace until she reached where she reckoned the hand had been. After taking a large gulp of air, she dived. It was hard to see. As soon as she was a few feet below, everything became darker, but she swore she saw something move ahead of her.

Heck, it could be a seal. It could be anything. Who knew? But Catriona made for it, pushing hard through the water. Then she reached out with a hand and touched something. That was human. That was a hand as well. But it slipped from her, so she swam on almost blindly, and then she hit something.

Her head collided with a body. She wrapped her arms around it and started kicking hard for the surface. It felt like it would never come. How deep down was she? Surely not far. She was diving without any oxygen or anything. The pressure of the sea did not feel that strong. Why was it taking so long to get up? And then she broke the surface.

Catriona opened her mouth, sucking in as much air as she could. She looked into the face of Fragrance Paradise. The woman's eyes were closed and Cat was unsure what condition she was in.

'We are coming!' It was the voice of Captain Jollye. 'Over there, Limpet. Move it.'

Cat continued to kick her legs, trying to hold the surface. It took Captain Jollye a good thirty seconds to bring the boat alongside, and then another thirty seconds to get hold of Fragrance Paradise and bring her into the rib. Then she reached down for Catriona.

Catriona kicked hard, throwing herself inside the rib. Landing on top of Fragrance Paradise, she spun off and sat down in a seat.

The captain looked at their casualty. 'We need to get her

onto the boat quick,' said Captain Jollye. She stood up and shouted to the women on the glacier. 'You will have to stay there. I will be back in ten minutes for you. But we need to get this girl inside.' The captain took off her coat and threw it at Catriona. 'Put that on. You will need it.'

She was not joking. Catriona was shivering now, the wind whipping over her wet body. But she had pulled Fragrance up, and Cat thought she saw the woman breathe. Then there was no time to think before the rib was bouncing as fast as it could over the water towards the cruise ship.

The captain was on the radio calling ahead and by the time they had come alongside, Scott Jones and Chris Denny were there to carry Fragrance inside. Captain Jollye then shouted to Limpet to return and get the others stuck on the glacier. Jollye then helped Catriona back onto the cruise ship.

'Are you okay?' asked the captain, looking into Catriona's eyes. 'You have been in the cold. Can you get into a shower? Can you warm yourself up?'

Catriona did not want to be an imposition when she knew the captain had a casualty to deal with. So, she simply nodded and made for her own room. She could feel the chill coming, and as she fell inside her own cabin door, Cat struggled over to the shower. Pressing it on, Cat stripped off and stood inside shivering before feeling the hot water run across her.

It was good. She could feel her fingers again, her body recovering. But then she wondered, *How does somebody like Fragrance end up in the water and so far away? There were only six people on the glacier. How did she fall in with no one noticing? A man dies in a gun accident. He was seen walking. A woman's cabin is turned over, and someone ends up in the water on a lonely glacier.* Something was afoot. Catriona was going to find out what it was, and it would not be a half-arsed effort like Tiff was doing.

# Chapter 7

Catriona changed back in her cabin once the chill had come out of her body. She exited the room looking for everyone else. She thought Tiff might have made the effort to come and see her to check if she was all right, but in going out to the open deck she saw Tiff pointing at the glacier and explaining to the captain what she thought had happened.

'Captain, how is she? Is Paradise all right?'

'She's come around nicely,' said the captain. 'I think she's going to be fine. But she took quite a chill. I think she was starting to freeze up there. I doubt she would've got back to the surface without you. She probably owes you her life.'

'It was nothing really.'

'It was definitely something,' said Tiff. 'Seems to me like she was pushed in.'

'But you just hold that talk,' said the captain. 'That's too much. There's no reason to say that. You've got a suspicious mind, but you've got no evidence. I'm not going to have people running around here amuck stirring things up when we need to stay calm. I'm the authority on the boat, Tiffany. Me and me only. So, enough. Catriona, kindly keep your niece in check.'

Catriona slid around behind Tiff, put her hands on her

shoulders and looked at the captain. 'Absolutely. She'll be no bother to you. Don't worry.' With that, the captain nodded and disappeared off back inside the vessel.

'Some help you were. You keep me in check, will you? Stop me from looking at this.'

'Shush. You're going about it all the wrong way.'

'I think something is up.'

'I agree with you. But if all you're going to do is start upsetting people, you're going to end up getting silenced yourself. Think about it, Tiff.'

'It's all pretty obvious. I just don't understand why anybody shot Ernest. If indeed he did get shot. And why would you cover up being shot? It just seems crazy. I need to get into that owner's cabin again. I will look inside the bag. You said he was dead. Are you sure he was dead?'

'Tiff, I am not sure of anything. I was thinking about this, and I don't know what it's like when somebody dies. It's only Luigi I saw.'

'And his wasn't even much of a death, was it?'

Catriona stared at Tiff. 'Thanks. I'm sorry my husband's death disappointed you.'

'What?' asked Tiff. 'Well, it wasn't, was it? He just sort of collapsed. It wasn't much of a death at all.'

Fighting back the tears, Catriona looked at her niece. This is when it was hard. Tiff didn't mean to be cruel. She wasn't intentionally nasty. But she had absolutely no idea what anybody else felt. But try as hard as she did to feel sorry for Tiff at this point, all Cat felt was anger. 'Come on, we need to go and see our friend Paradise. See how she is. And you need to get in your head why somebody wanted to kill her.'

'There weren't many of us out there. There was you, Mrs

Bridge, the captain, and Limpet. No one else. Somebody must have done it amongst us. It wasn't me and the captain, we weren't close.'

'I think Tara was up ahead, spouting on about something. The only one who ever got behind me was . . . It must have been Mrs Bridge.'

'But why?' asked Catriona. 'I don't know any good reason. Come on. Let's find Paradise and see if we can get her alone.'

On finding First officer Jones, he advised Cat that Paradise was in her cabin recovering. Catriona thanked him for the information and made to visit Paradise, but he grabbed her arm.

'They say you dived in to save her. That was quite something, wasn't it? There's a lot to you that's not obvious on a first look. Quite a woman you are. Certainly, someone I want to get to know an awful lot closer. Does your niece always sleep in the cabin? You can't get her away at all, can you? I could pop in tonight.'

Catriona felt he was very forward and as much as she liked the man, with everything that was going on, she certainly didn't want to trust anyone. 'Why can't we go to yours?' she asked.

'Problem is, the captain doesn't like it, doesn't like people down in the crew quarters. But she doesn't mind us playing a bit, obviously as long as it's not in everyone's face. So how about it? You think you can get Tiff to get out, at least for an hour or two?'

'There's a lot going on at the moment, Scott. Let's just . . . let's just see, okay? I want to go and check on Paradise. Make sure she's okay. I felt like I nearly lost her there. It's a good job I was just in time.'

Catriona waited for Scott to agree, but he didn't. His mind seemed to be somewhere else when she made the comment. 'Okay, well, we'll see,' said Catriona. Watching the man's face, she saw it suddenly break concentration and come back to her. He nodded as she left him, making her way back to the guest quarters and to the cabin of Heinrich and Fragrance.

Knocking on the door, Catriona stood back wondering if she was being a bit impertinent rushing in on a woman who just survived death. The door opened and Heinrich, smiling through his large white beard, reached out a hand.

'I need to thank you. You have saved my precious Fragrance, my precious Paradise. It was you that dived in to save her. Thank you.'

'It's not a problem. I'm sure anybody else would have done it. But I was wondering, could I just see her? Just to make sure she's okay.'

'The captain said she was to have her peace, but I guess so. I think we owe you that much. Come on, step inside.' Catriona entered the room that looked remarkably similar to her own. Tiff followed, almost peering over Catriona's shoulder as she saw the blonde-haired woman lying in bed.

'Is she asleep, Heinrich? Maybe we should come back another time.' In her ear she heard a whisper. 'She's not asleep,' said Tiff. 'Those eyes are partly open.'

The eyes suddenly flipped fully open. 'It's fine. You can stay,' said Paradise. 'I know you are here to see me, but I'm telling Heinrich, I don't trust anyone.'

'As long as you're sure you didn't slip,' said the German professor. 'What reason on earth would Mrs Bridge have to do anything like that to you?'

'You think it was Mrs Bridge?' said Catriona, surprised.

'Well, at the end of the day, who else could it be?' said Paradise. 'You were away with the captain. Your sister was up ahead with Miss Limpet. Mrs Bridge was the only one near me.'

'But did you actually see her push you in?'

'No, I didn't,' said Paradise. 'But there wasn't anyone else on the glacier.'

'That's not true, is it?' said Tiff. Everyone else in the room turned and stared at her.

'Who else was on it? Who else was on the glacier?' said Catriona.

'Well, I don't know,' said Tiff. 'But obviously someone. If Mrs Bridge has no idea or no reason to shove her in, somebody else must have had one, and that means somebody else was on the glacier.'

Catriona stared at Tiff, and then slowly shook her head. 'Not helpful.' And with that, she turned back to Paradise. 'Do you have any medical conditions? Anything that could have caused you to fall in?'

Heinrich gave a cough. 'She has fainted before and has had episodes, but Paradise is saying that she definitely stayed awake the whole time before she went in. She says she felt a push.'

'And you don't believe me, do you?' said Paradise. 'He doesn't.'

'Well, I want to and I don't want to,' said Heinrich. 'That means somebody wanted to kill you. I find that hard to believe. Maybe me or some of the things I've said in the past, but not you. And you have to remember after having the treatment, the hypnosis for falling down all those times. It really is something that's quite possible. Maybe you felt you were pushed. Maybe the feet going from under you felt like something.'

'I was pushed, Heinrich. I know I was pushed.'

'Easy,' said Catriona. 'It's not an easy situation for anyone. So, let's just work on a premise that you were pushed. It would have to be Mrs Bridge.'

'Or somebody else getting onto the glacier,' said Tiff. 'Why does everyone think that's not a thing that's going to happen?'

'Tiff, we were on a boat. We were yards away from the boat, hundreds of yards. They would have had to get into the water, get over, jump up on the glacier, run over, shove Paradise here into the water then dive back in, swim away and get back to the boat.'

'And?' said Tiff. 'Sounds perfectly feasible to me.'

'And why?' said Catriona. 'Why?'

'I'm working on that,' she says. 'A lot depends on why someone would want to kill Mr Hughes, guns going off for no reason. But why also would the crew want to cover it up? Do you think they were annoyed with their owner?'

'Well, I don't know.' said Catriona. 'But the captain has been known to be all alone with him. Maybe he spurned her, maybe he wasn't for her anymore.'

'Okay,' said Heinrich. 'But that doesn't tell me why someone is trying to kill Fragrance. Can you explain that to me? Why would someone would want to kill this lovely creature of mine?'

'Heinrich, I'm not a pet,' retorted Fragrance.

'But you are under threat. Now rest up. I think we've had enough excitement. I think we should shut the door and rest up. I'm sorry, Contessa, but can I ask you and your niece to leave? I think we just need a bit of rest.'

'But, of course,' said Catriona. 'I think we'll go and ask around a few other people. Things have got a little strange, but

I'm glad to see you're okay.' Catriona turned away. She heard Paradise getting out of the bed. The woman was wearing a long t-shirt and with no embarrassment walked up to Catriona, simply flung her arms around her, and hugged her tight.

'Thank you. Thank you for what you did. You could have died doing it.'

'Highly unlikely, as she's quite a good swimmer. She also understands how to swim in cold water and frankly, she was probably the best chance you had.'

Catriona raised her head and looked at Tiff, giving a gentle shake of the head. 'Not the time, Tiff.' Tiff gave a look back indicating 'what have I done wrong', before leaving the room. Watching Paradise return to the bed, Catriona thanked Heinrich for his time but was again shaken by the hand profusely. 'Thank you', said the German professor. 'By the way, your niece. She's quite special, no?'

'More special than you can believe,' said Catriona. 'But special needs a lot of looking after.' With that, she departed the room and made her way down to the stateroom feeling peckish. The tables were set up in the middle of the stateroom, and around the edges were cold meats and various pastries that could be taken at any time of the day. Tiff was already in the stateroom sitting down with a cup of tea and opposite her was Demi Forsythe, Mr Hughes's PA. Catriona poured herself a cup of coffee and then shook her head as she heard Tiff begin to question Miss Forsythe.

'I guess you'll be out of a job then. You're going to have to start looking for something when you get back to land.' Catriona saw the wide eyes of Demi Forsythe.

'Well, yes, I was extremely fortunate. Landed on my feet with Mr Hughes, a very generous man, but someone will have to take over. I'm sure they'll need a PA as well.' Unlike most of the guests who were sitting around in casual clothing during the day, Demi Forsythe always looked like a PA. At the moment, she was wearing a sharp skirt and a blouse, but the mascara in her eyes had run. 'It's just going to be hard finding someone like him. It felt like he was more than a boss.'

'You were having an affair with him?' asked Tiff.

'No, no, no,' said Demi. 'He was just a close friend. I travelled so far with him and saw him going about his business, making deals, meeting people. I got to know him, understand him. Even with the women he met, sometimes he would ask me whether they were good enough for him or not, which is a bit of a funny question. But he had no one else. He only ever turned to me.'

Catriona brought her coffee over to the table and sat down beside Demi. 'Did he ever have a special woman who he wanted to marry?'

'Oh, no,' said Demi. 'He was never like that. Women weren't a commodity, but they were definitely not a lifelong commitment. He felt they got the best of him and I think most of them did.'

'You always get weird ones though, don't you?'

'Mainly get weird men, though Heinrich is something else.'

'Are you talking about the beard?' said Tiffany. Once again Catriona's eyes rolled.

'No,' said Demi. 'Not at all. He was just always going on to Mr Hughes, explaining what he was doing wrong in life. Just because he's older, he felt he could just demand things of him.'

'But they had some sort of business relationship then?' said Catriona. 'I'm just confused about how everyone here seems to know him. Everyone seemed to have a link to Mr Hughes, except me and Tiff.'

'Well, that's because you were very last minute. There was a cancellation, and he liked the idea of having a Contessa on board. He said to me, "It's a sort of royalty, isn't it?" He can have any number of business people, he knew them all. But getting to know the Royal families, getting to know people with titles, I think that was becoming something for him. And if I'm honest, I think he wanted to know you. He knew you'd just been widowed. Like I say, he liked the company of good women.'

'Well, he would probably have been frankly disappointed then,' said Tiff. Catriona raised her eyes and looked at her niece. Every time somebody said something nice about Cat, she had to jump in. There were appearances to keep up here. Tiffany didn't understand that.

'I'm sure he would have been quite delightful,' said Catriona. 'So did Mrs Bridge know him well?' Demi noted.

'Very well. An item once, certainly business dealings. I always wondered with Mrs Bridge. I always felt she knew more about him than she let on.'

'What business dealings did they have?' asked Catriona.

'Well, he invested in her fitness clubs, got her up to where she was. He was the one who suggested she should be the front image for the clubs. "The middle-aged woman who would steer the ship instead of some young bimbo," he said. Most of his women were younger than him, but she was older. There was something about her that fascinated him.'

'Why did they split up?' asked Catriona.

'That's just the way he was. He never wanted to be tied down.'

'Wouldn't have done much for you then,' said Tiff, looking

at Catriona. 'Catriona likes them, falls for them, and marries them. Of course, Luigi had a bad heart, but he was a good match. Most of his family didn't like him either.'

Catriona stood up, excused herself from Demi Forsythe, and walked outside. Standing on the railing, she looked at the icy surroundings. How long would Tiff be like this? Well, forever. But as much as she pretended to be indignant about what Tiff had said, really, she just wanted to get outside and start chewing over things. There was a connection between everyone then. Demi had said as much. Catriona would need to get deeper into that. *Why were rooms being broken into? Why did someone try to kill Paradise?* She saw the shadow of her niece before the girl ambled up to her side.

'It's becoming fun, isn't it?' said Tiff.

'I think it is,' said Catriona. 'But we need to be careful. Paradise didn't die today, but she was meant to. I don't know why but we need to find out.' With that, she turned around and took Tiff's hand. 'But we don't want to die in the process.'

# Chapter 8

The rest of the day was quite subdued, but the captain announced that dinner that night would continue to be a formal affair. Once again, Catriona found herself wanting to dress up and play the part. The first officer, Scott Jones, called by at six o'clock asking if she was coming to dinner that evening. He offered to escort her, but Catriona refused, saying she would take Tiff with her as she felt the girl needed company. The man looked a little hurt, but Catriona decided that if he really felt anything for her, he would work a lot harder. As she walked down to dinner, Catriona was pulled to one side and stared up into the face of the chef, Ivan Popov.

'Be incredibly careful,' he said. 'They are all in it, you have to know they are all in it.' Catriona went to ask him why, but someone tapped her on the shoulder.

'Oh,' said Catriona, 'it's you.'

The face of Scott Jones smiled at her. 'I may not be able to walk you to dinner, but now that you are here, let me offer you your seat.' She nodded, but she saw that first officer glance at the chef. 'Was he bothering you? You really should not be coming up here, Popov, It's not your place. The chef, Miss Limpet, and Mr Denny are servers,' Jones explained. 'It is only the first officer and the captain who can get to sit with the guests.'

'Well, quite an honour for me? I was quite taken with her today on the glacier before our little incident. She certainly knows how to let her hair down when she wants to.'

'Oh, the captain knows what she is doing,' said the first officer.

'Have you two worked together for long?' asked Catriona.

'Long enough, but here, let me.' Catriona took the seat which had been pulled out for her, and First Officer Jones sat beside her. Tiff at this time had made a move, clearly wanting to put some distance between her aunt and herself, possibly for the investigation. She was sitting beside Tyrrell Kopeck, who was positioned at the far end of the table. Catriona was afforded one of the seats closest to the captain, who reached forward and touched Cat's hand.

'Are you okay with your niece being that far away? I realise you are a calming influence on her. I wouldn't want her to get carried away tonight.'

'I think she will be fine and if she is not, I will attend to it,' said Catriona, 'but thank you for your concern.' Beside Catriona was Jack Fogherty. The man was quiet, not engaging in conversation with anyone else. Opposite him was Heinrich with Paradise. The woman looked pale after her ordeal and with her blonde hair, she seemed to lack any colour at all. Heinrich seemed gruff, not answering any questions, and as the rest of the guests filed into their seats, he seemed impatient for his dinner.

As the starter arrived, drinks were served, but tonight Catriona was going easy. Taking a glass of white wine, she sipped it slowly, despite constant urgings from the first officer by her side to drink up more.

The captain cleared her throat and then asked Paradise how she was. Before she could answer, Heinrich turned and stared at the woman.

'How do you think she is, dear Captain? Someone tried to kill her today.'

'Hardly,' said the captain. 'That's quite a jump to make. No one saw her fall into the water. Not even Mrs Bridge and she was the closest. We saw no one else on that glacier. I fear your partner must have had some sort of incident.'

Heinrich shook his head. 'I don't like your inference. Unlike myself, Fragrance is fighting fit, but today we nearly lost her. I am not happy and I am keeping an eye on everyone here, everyone indeed.'

'I'm not sure I like your tone,' said Tyrrell Kopeck. 'Some of us were sat here on the boat and had nothing to do with it.'

'You're absolutely right,' said Jack Fogherty. 'I was sitting over here, nothing to do with it.'

'Just because someone was not seen on the glacier does not mean that they were not there,' said Tiffany. 'That is quite elementary.'

*Here we go*, thought Catriona. *She is going to try to put on her detective voice, pretend she is one of the characters from the books. That is all we need.* Catriona cleared her throat. 'Tiff, no need to get involved.'

'I think someone needs to get involved,' said Heinrich. 'We should be turning this boat into the nearest port, having the police on board to investigate.'

'That is my decision, professor. At this time, I feel it is not warranted,' said the captain.

'What sort of captain are you, anyway? Look at you sitting there,' said Heinrich. 'You are not a guest and you are dressed like a woman ready for a night out. I'm not happy about this and we should be making for port.'

'I didn't pay a small fortune to come here and then head for port,' said Sarah Gosling. 'And I was burgled! I still want to stay so there is no way we are heading for port.'

First Officer Jones stood up. 'Can we just have a bit of calm, please? The captain has made her decision.'

With that, the captain stood up. 'Thank you, first officer. Before we have any more rancour around the dinner table, understand that I have made the decision. We shall carry on with our trip and in a couple of weeks we shall arrive at port and the authorities will come on board to take away Mr Hughes's body. Until then, let us stay civilised.'

The professor shook his head. 'This is not civilised. We would not do this in Germany.'

'You are testing my patience,' said the captain. 'I have offered you every courtesy and sympathy for what happened, but please do not talk of things that are not true.'

Fragrance Paradise stood up suddenly, knocking her glass over which smashed on the floor. She stared around the table. 'Someone pushed me,' she shouted, 'someone pushed me into the water and if it were not for that woman over there,' she said pointing at the Contessa, 'I would be dead. So, let us stop these shenanigans; let us stop this pretence that we are on a jolly little cruise. Someone tried to kill me; someone may have killed Mr Hughes.'

'Sit down,' said Tyrrell. With that, Heinrich stood up and marched around the table. First Officer Jones stood up to try to stop him, but the German reached for the movie actor, clutching him by the throat. 'Stop, show some respect to my partner.'

'Partner?' said Sarah Gosling. 'Look at her; she could be your granddaughter. It's disgusting.' And with that, Fragrance marched out of the room. Heinrich threw a punch and caught the movie star on the jaw, tipping him back off his seat. Mr Denny ran in and with First Officer Jones, they pulled Heinrich away from him.

The captain clapped her hands. 'I think that is enough for the evening, gentlemen. Kindly retire to your rooms and I shall have some food brought to you.' The big German stared at the captain, lifting a finger, wagging it at her. But he said nothing and then strode from the room.

'Well, that all got a little lively, didn't it?' said Jack Fogherty. 'Wasn't expecting that.' Catriona's eyes looked at Mrs Bridge at the end of the table. Unlike the rest of the guests, she neither seemed shocked nor disturbed by what had happened. But the woman watched everything very closely. Mr Denny and Miss Limpet ran around tidying up the table and sweeping the broken glass off the floor.

'Bring out some more wine,' shouted the Captain. 'Let us have an evening of it and forget this nonsense.' Tiff went to speak, but Catriona caught her eye and raised a finger. This was a time to observe and not get involved. The rest of the meal was eaten in silence, with only the odd comment and a compliment for the food. Catriona was pondering about being taken aside at the start of the evening by the chef and wondered if she could get to speak to him again.

'This beef is quite delicious. I was wondering, would you mind, captain, if I pop down to give my thanks to your chef? It is quite excellent.'

'I am afraid Chef will be off tonight,' said the captain. 'He works hard throughout the day so I tend to give him the rest of the night off, once the meals are all prepared.'

'Regardless, I shall pop down and have a look,' said Catriona, and stood up to a glare from the captain. 'Don't worry,' said Catriona, 'I'm sure I can find my way down. I won't touch anything. Just going to say thank you.'

'I will accompany you,' said the first officer.

'No, it's fine. I am a Contessa, after all. I think I can handle myself.' And with that Catriona stepped out of the stateroom through one of the doors at the rear from which the food normally arrived.

There were a series of small steps down into the galley. Catriona looked around, hoping to spot the chef still at work. Walking through, she saw everything was cleared away, pans set to one side. The man was clearly good at what he did. But there would be more cutlery to come through. She wondered if he was responsible for that, or maybe Mr Denny and Miss Limpet simply put them in the dishwashers that were available.

Wandering on through the galley, Catriona found a door that led up to what must be the crew's quarters. As she walked through, she saw signs for the Captain's cabin, the First Officer, and three smaller cabins. One had its door open and she could smell a cigarette. Popping her head in, she saw no one and then there was a hoarse voice coming from the end of the corridor.

'What are you doing looking in there?' It was the chef.

Catriona pulled her head back out. 'You spoke to me earlier; you said I should watch them. Who should I watch?'

The man lurched down the corridor. 'All of them. Do not you know? All of them.'

'All the guests,' asked Catriona, 'or all the crew?'

'It does not matter,' said the man. 'They will find you, too; you are not meant to be here. He was not going to bother with you. You were just interesting. Maybe he is still interested.'

'He is dead,' said Catriona. 'Mr Hughes is dead. But he walks, Miss Gosling's said he walked.'

'Who do you believe?' laughed the man. And it was then that Catriona saw the bottle in the man's hand. It looked like a vodka bottle, but there was not much liquid left.

'Come with me,' said the man and staggered back down the corridor. Catriona followed and he opened the door to the small piece of outside deck. It was on the extreme rear of the boat and he pointed with his hand out towards the ice floe.

'You could swim. You saved the girl; that was good. I could not swim—I would not have saved her.' English was clearly not the man's first language. And the way he was slurring his speech was making it exceedingly difficult for Catriona to understand.

'But you told me to beware. Beware of who?'

'Did they swim?' he said. 'Did they swim across? Tonight, I heard, she said she fell in, the German girl. I like she survived. She is nice, nice to look at. When I bring you drinks, I looked at her, not at you. This job is good when you get nice people on board. Not good now.'

'Who is not nice on board then?'

But the man was just looking off into the distance. 'They swam across. They swam like you. Maybe you need to look at how they swim. Yes?'

'Is he bothering you?' It was First Officer Jones. 'The captain said I should come down. Unfortunately, our chef likes a little tipple after he is finished his work for the day. Is not that right, Mr Popov?'

'I like my drink, that is what I like,' said the chef. 'But you go, I thank you.'

'It was a lovely meal,' said Catriona. 'You really can cook.' With that, she reached forward, gave the man a peck on the cheek. As she stepped back, he stepped forward, kissing her on the cheek. And then she heard a quiet whisper, 'Be careful.'

'Hey, steady on, Popov.'

'It is okay,' said Catriona. 'It is an Italian custom. I am the Contessa, he understands. He's not meaning anything by it—just being very polite.'

'Does that mean I get to kiss you in that fashion as well?'

'Only when I thanked you for something,' said Catriona. 'Please show me the way back and we will leave the man to his drink.' As the first officer made his way back along the corridor and then to the door to the kitchen, Catriona looked back. She watched Mr Popov slump on the floor. The man knew something but he was in no state to talk to. When back in the stateroom, the captain asked how the chef had been and Catriona replied, 'delightful.' The stateroom was nearly empty, and it seemed that last night's frivolities were not going to happen tonight.

'I believe your niece has already made her way upstairs. Mr Fogherty was with her.'

'Well, Tiffany's her own woman. I think I shall retire too.'

'Let me escort you then,' said the first officer. Catriona was not entirely happy with this, but she thought it was probably the safer option.

'What a better way to end the evening.' She took his arm as he walked her up back to her cabin. Cat knocked on the door before opening it and saw Tiff's legs lying on the bed. 'I'm afraid Tiff's in. I think I will have to go off to bed now. But thank you for seeing me up.'

'Until another night then,' said Jack.

'Maybe,' said Catriona. And with that, she reached out and give him a peck on the cheek. He reached down and kissed her back.

'I like this Italian thing.' And with that, he walked off. What an idiot, thought Catriona. No idea how Italians do anything? As she went to close the door, she heard footsteps in the corridor. Quickly she glanced out and saw Jack Fogherty opening his door, with Tara Limpet following him inside. As Cat closed the door behind her, she wondered just what was going on. This crew seemed to get awfully familiar with the guests, even the deckhands.

'And how was your chef? Did you tell him how good the beef was?' asked Tiff.

'All he had was a warning to be careful. And he was drunk, muttering something about the swim. How to swim from here to the glacier. We need to check the suits.'

'Really,' said Tiff. 'Then maybe we need to go for a swim in the morning.'

# Chapter 9

Cat sat up in bed. She looked around for an indication of what time it was and noted that Tiff was also sitting up in bed, eyes glued on her phone.

'What are you doing? Do you know what time it is?'

'So? You're up, are you? Why are you asking me these questions?'

*Always the same old Tiff, question right back. Never a simple answer from her.* 'But what are you doing?' asked Cat.

'I thought we needed to start checking these people out, just who they are exactly. It's not the fastest Wi-Fi in the world, but at least we've got some sort of connection. It's taking me a while, but I'm working on it.'

'I doubt you're going to find anything that way,' said Cat. 'We need to get to know them better, need to get closer. But I'm worried, Tiff; I'm worried because the crew seem to be getting awfully close to people.'

'When you dress up like that, that's what happens,' said Tiff. 'Surprised he hasn't tried to bed you yet.'

'Oi, don't be so forward. I'm not some sort of tart running around here. I'm just looking classy. And besides, can you blame him? He's probably besotted by the Contessa thing.'

'That's not what you said earlier there; you said a lot of the crew are hanging about people—what do you mean?'

'Well, our dashing first officer seems to be very enamoured with me and I saw Jack Fogherty disappearing inside his cabin with Tara Limpet. Wouldn't be surprised if we have Mr Denny somewhere.'

'Harriet Bridge, that will be the one he'll be going for. Makes sense, doesn't it?' said Tiff. 'She's on her own—he's quite young. These older women like younger men, don't they? That's the way it happens.'

'It's not an episode of some soap opera, but you do wonder what she's doing out here on her own. It's interesting, Tiff. Tyrrell Kopeck was at it as well, but I think he's just a complete flirt. He's out for a good time, living off the money of Sarah Gosling. He seems to be getting away from her every opportunity he gets.'

'I never recognised any of his films,' said Tiff. 'I wonder, was he any good? Probably not.'

'But why would the crew be getting so close? That's one thing I'm noting, all except Mr Popov. He warned me. He warned me about them. But he was so drunk I don't know who he was talking about. Is it the crew? Or the guests? Certainly, Captain Jollye wants to keep all talk of our dead man walking closed down. You need to be more subtle, Tiff. I know that's asking a lot.'

'People need to hear things; they need to be told straight. There's no point being subtle.'

'There is if you're trying to investigate things and not want people to know. We need to get inside that cabin and see if he's really dead. Get you to have a look at him. I wouldn't know if he was dead or not.' Catriona became aware that Tiffany was looking straight at her, shaking her head as if Cat had said the most unbelievable thing going.

'How do you not know if someone is dead? You should have punched him, see if he sat up. I bet you didn't even try for a pulse, did you?'

'No, I didn't. I don't do dead bodies. They're all cold and lifeless. I'm full of life and fun, Tiff, not like you.'

'There's plenty of people who aren't the life and soul of the party who can recognise a dead body. Anyway, how are we going to get in? Do we do it at night?'

'Possibly, but not tonight. We need to think about this. Have you found anything though, on the internet, Tiff?'

'Well, actually I have. It seems that the people on board are intricately linked to Mr Hughes. Harriett Bridge was backed by him for fitness clubs. Professor Weber did some work in some environmental studies into a pipeline Mr Hughes was involved with. Sarah Gosling backed some money into that pipeline as well. Jack Fogherty's racing team is backed by Mr Hughes. I also think that somewhere Mr Hughes's company tried to put money into a TV movie. At some point, Hughes's money is always involved.'

'If you think about the crew, they're all employed by him, and our captain, Louise Jollye, is doing more than just being a captain. She was getting very jolly with him from what she said to me. Popov is the exception. I need to talk more to him as well. Maybe I should write this down.'

'Don't be silly,' said Tiff. 'You write things down, they know what you're doing; keep it in your head. If you can't do that, tell me everything. I'll keep it in my head.'

'Stop trying to make out like you're Sherlock.'

A scream cut the air, and both women looked at each other before leaping out of bed. Catriona grabbed her dressing gown, wrapping it around her. Tiff simply opened the door in her pyjamas, stepping outside. The door to Harriet Bridge's cabin was lying open and Tiff ran inside, followed by Catriona. The woman was kneeling on the floor, distraught. 'What's up?' asked Catriona. She heard more people trying to cram through the door behind her.

'There,' said Harriet. 'Over there. The safe has been broken into, and I saw him. He was right here. I saw him.'

'Saw who?' asked Catriona.

The woman was white as a sheet. 'Ernest. Ernest was in here. He looked at me and simply shook his head before walking out that door. What does he want with me, huh?' From behind her, Catriona heard another scream. Turning, she saw Sarah Gosling becoming frantic and beginning to shout at Tyrrell Kopeck.

'I told you it was a lie. I told you. You stupid man, sitting there telling me I was an idiot—all the money had gone to my head.'

'What's going on?' It was a women's voice. Authoritative, but it wasn't the captain. Catriona watched Tara Limpet walk through the room. She was still dressed in her uniform, but it looked like it had been hastily thrown on. Behind her, Catriona saw a smiling Jack Fogherty.

'He's been about again—Earnest. Earnest has been on the run,' said Harriet. Catriona took the women in her arms, kneeling beside her and hugging her tight.

'Right, we need to clear this room. Contessa, by all means, attend to Mrs Bridge. If everyone else would kindly leave the room and go to your own cabins, I'll bring the captain down for a word later.'

'To do what?' said the Professor. 'How do we know you're

not covering something up?  It's another person hurt, their belongings broken into, and I nearly lost Fragrance earlier. What is going on?'

Tara Limpet started moving towards the assembled crowd at the door, hands up, trying to push back a pocket of air between her and them, moving them back into the corridor.

'We won't solve any of this now. Back to your cabins. Lock the doors, and I'll get the captain to speak to you. That goes for you, too, Ms Munroe.'

Catriona looked up and saw Tiff was already making her way towards the safe.

'That's a bad idea, Ms Limpet; best if Tiff stays with me—it's just she can be awkward.'

Anyone else hearing this would have turned round and stared incredulously at the speaker of the words, but Tiff completely ignored what Catriona was saying and continued to look around the safe.

'Very well,' said Tara Limpet, 'But keep her away from touching too much stuff. The captain might want to investigate.'

'I shall touch nothing except with my pencil.  Now please clear the room.'

Despite the situation, Catriona nearly burst out laughing at Tiff's comments. She was acting as if she were some sort of senior detective, and Cat wondered how this would play out on the arrival of the captain. It took five minutes for the captain to arrive, and she was accompanied by her first officer, Scott Jones. On entering the cabin, the captain looked around before marching back out of it. Meanwhile, First Officer Jones came down to Mrs Bridge, kneeling before her, asking if she was okay. The woman was sniffing, but she nodded. He next looked up at Catriona.

'You really are quite kind, aren't you, but I think we can take it from here.' A hand shot out onto Catriona's arm.

'I'd like the Contessa to stay,' said Mrs Bridge. 'I don't feel that safe.'

'Do you know if there's anything missing?' asked Catriona, but the women simply held her head in her hands. 'If you could give us a bit of space, Scott, I'll take Harriet over to her safe to see if she recognises if anything is missing.' Scott reluctantly stepped back and Catriona led the woman over.

The safe was a simple design with a numbered code, only big enough to hold maybe a small folder. Inside were a few papers and some jewellery.

'Anything missing?' asked Catriona. 'Please, Harriet, take a look. We need to know.' Harriet wiped her eyes, bent down, and started rifling through the papers.

'No, it's all here; my jewellery is all here; his paperwork is here, not that it was that important—it's all here.' Then the woman turned and looked straight at Cat's face, 'But so was he. He's dead—they said he's dead.'

'Just calm down,' said Cat, 'We'll work this out.'

'We don't need to work anything out,' said Tiff. 'He's alive. He's walking on the ship and he's alive. The man never died in the first place.'

Then came a shout from outside the cabin. 'Would you shut that niece of yours up? It's not what people need at the moment.' Captain Jollye entered the room, dressed in her full uniform and with a face like thunder. 'I said before, you don't need to be spreading that sort of nonsense about.'

'Tiff, just keep a lid on it, please,' said Catriona. 'Look captain, Mrs Bridge has had quite a shock. I think we should leave her alone.' Again, her hand shot out onto Catriona's arm.

'No,' said Mrs Bridge, 'I want you to stay. I want you to stay in the cabin with me. You're a good person; he didn't know you—you're good. I can trust you.'

'The whole crew is here. I think there's plenty of people you can trust.' The hand squeezed tighter on Cat's arm and Mrs Bridge looked straight into her eyes.

'No, there isn't. Stay here and your niece can stay, too. I don't care how she talks.'

'Well, if nothing is missing,' said Captain Jollye, 'and all we have is this reported sighting of my dead boss walking around, I don't see there's that much to investigate. Maybe you've left it open, Mrs Bridge. Have you been taking anything?' With that, the captain marched into the small en-suite. On exiting, she took Cat aside and advised her that Mrs Bridge seemed to be doing some quite strong drugs.

'Maybe the whole thing is just in her imagination, especially after Sarah Gosling set her off. That woman doesn't know what she's done. I reckon the first one was too much alcohol, and this one is too many drugs—been seeing things. You know I showed you; he's dead and wrapped in a body bag. I wish he weren't, but he is.'

A voice came over Catriona's shoulder, 'Cat wouldn't know a dead body from a mannequin. You could have got somebody sensible to see if the man were dead.'

The captain put her hands on her hips, staring forcibly at Tiff. 'You need to stop that. You need to stop raising up this nonsense.'

'And I will if you let me see the body. Take me to it. Let me see his cold hands. Let me check his pulse.'

'If it's going to make you happy, I'll take you,' said Captain Jollye. 'I'll take you and I'll show you him, but after that, you must stop this nonsense.'

'Fine,' said Tiff. 'But if I find him and he's not dead, what are you going to do?'

'Be outside in ten minutes,' said the captain. 'I'm going to show you this once and for all.'

# Chapter 10

Harriet Bridge was not happy about letting Catriona go with Tiffany and the captain. As Catriona went to leave her, the woman grabbed her arm, pulling her back and hugging her tight. She seemed a far cry from the figure she had recognised the other day. The glasses were off, the mascara was running, and the long thick wave of brown hair that usually swung so happily on her shoulders seemed limp and lacklustre.

'It'll be okay,' said Cat. 'We'll be back very shortly; we just need to go look at something.'

'Can't one of you go?' said Harriet. 'Please stay, I don't trust anyone else.'

'I know you don't but neither do I and I'm not letting my niece go alone. We'll be back in about ten minutes and then we'll stay here. Maybe I can get someone else to stand in front of the door while you wait.'

Catriona thought for a moment about how best to do this. She could ask the first officer, Scott Jones, to stay behind, stand outside the door, but she wasn't sure she trusted him either. Going to Mr Popov was also probably a bad idea. Or maybe a combination of crew and guest would be best. Still in her dressing gown, Cat approached the first officer, taking him by the hand and leading him outside of the cabin.

Cat flashed her eyes and watched a pleasing smile on the man's face. 'Can I ask you a favour?' she said. 'She's not feeling the best, Mrs Bridge, and she wants me to stay with her, but we have some business with the captain to attend to. So, I was wondering if you could stand guard outside here and alongside Mr Fogherty? Just for ten or fifteen minutes. I'd ask you to do it on your own but I'm afraid she's suspicious of everyone, bit overwrought that woman but I know I can trust you,' said Cat. Inside she was not trusting the man at all but he seemed to be compliant with her suggestion.

'Of course, and maybe later you could see fit for having a word with me in your own cabin? Tiff could stay with Mrs Bridge.'

'I'll see what I can do, but Tiff is a character in her own right, not easy to handle. That would be a lot to dump on the woman who's in such a state as Mrs Bridge.' And with that, Cat reached up and gave the man a peck on the cheek before shuffling down the corridor and rapping the door of Jack Fogherty. The man answered in a dressing gown and when Cat put her request to him, he seemed fairly happy.

'Not too long though, I need to get back to my sleep. Unfortunately, I didn't sleep much beforehand, a little restless.' He had a grin on his face and from what she'd seen earlier, Cat believed he hadn't had a quiet night.

When Cat returned to Mrs Bridge's cabin, she explained the situation. The woman seemed fairly happy with the idea of two guards outside her door. 'I won't be long,' said Cat. 'I think this is the best thing. Tiff and I need to find out what's going on.' There was a call from outside the door and it opened to reveal the captain still dressed in her immaculate uniform, 'If you'll come this way, Contessa, we'll deal with our business now.'

With that, Cat grabbed Tiff, dragging her out of the door and following the captain along to the owner's quarters. Cat had been here before and when the door was opened, she recognised the same cabin undisturbed with the black bag lying on the bed.

'If we can have some dignity about this, it'll be much appreciated,' said the captain. 'If you both would like to come over.' Captain Jollye shut the door behind her and then walked around to the far side of the bed, reaching down and taking hold of the black bag in one hand and the zip in the other. 'If you haven't seen this before, it can be quite a shock. I hope your niece is up to it.' With that, she pulled the zip down, letting the bag fall open to reveal the face of Earnest Hughes. Just as before, it was pale. There was little emotion, but Tiff instinctively reached down to try to grab an eyelid. A hand shot across from the captain. 'What are you doing? You can't touch him. We don't want to disturb anything. The police wouldn't appreciate that.'

'I need to get a good look. I need to check he's dead.'

'He's lying in a black body bag. Look at the colour of him. What more do you want?'

Tiff turned around, touching Cat by the shoulder, 'We need to find out, check his pulse. Have a look at him properly.'

'Where's the weapon?' asked Cat. 'You said the weapon went off incorrectly, injured and killed him. Whereabouts did you say it hit him? I can't see any markings on his face?'

'It's further down in his stomach,' said the captain. 'It's not a pleasant sight, so I haven't pulled the bag down too far. There's also the issue that things might come out. You really don't want to see it.' She began to sniff.

'But the gun,' said Cat, 'I appreciate this is not a good time for you but is the gun in the room as well?'

'It's in the cupboard,' said the captain.

'May I see it?'

'Of course, if you come over here with me.' As the captain stepped in front of her, Cat turned around and gave a nod to Tiff, following the captain quietly across the floor. As the captain opened the cupboard to reveal a gun inside, Cat flipped her head right and saw Tiff reaching down into the black bag. But the captain turned suddenly.

'Would you come over here? Just leave him alone. I think it's enough I've gone through, without this.' With that, she started to cry. 'I've had to take him this far on a boat. I really don't need to be messed about by your kind. Please, Contessa, get hold of your niece.' Cat waved across, urging Tiff to come and stand beside her. Tiff shook her head, so Catriona ran over, grabbed her, and dragged her back.

Meanwhile, the captain pulled out the gun, a small rifle. 'As you can see, it's exploded here, gone wrong, blowing back into the side of him. We tried to save him, but it looked like a part of it had gone up into his heart. There was nothing we could do. I had to stand there and just watch him die. I'm sorry. Forgive me,' said Jollye, as the tears flowed down her cheeks, 'But I think that's it. We'll need to go. I hope you're satisfied now.'

'Eminently so,' said Cat, 'Aren't we?' Tiff went to shake her head, but Catriona grabbed her arm. 'No, Tiff, we are done. Now let's not have any more of this nonsense.'

Tiff's eyes were furious. 'It's not nonsense. It's not nonsense.' The Captain stepped forward and slapped Tiff across the face. 'Sorry, but she needs to stop. Every time she says it, I see him. Every time she goes on, it hurts. You're a widow. You must understand.'

'Apologise. We'll wait outside.' And with that, Cat turned, grabbed Tiff by the arm and marched into the outside corridor. When the captain joined them a minute later, Cat watched her close the door. 'We keep it isolated. Nobody else has been in there except us,' said the captain. 'He liked his privacy in life. I would like to keep it that way in death, so kindly please stay away from here and don't bother me anymore with this nonsense. I have a case of a thief on board. I think that's enough for me to deal with as well as the death of my friend.'

'My condolences for your loss,' said Catriona. 'You certainly loved him. I hope you find a way to cope and go on, and I'll certainly take care of my niece. Thank you for your cooperation, Captain. It's much appreciated, and if we can do anything else to help regarding the theft, then please don't hesitate to talk to me.' The Captain nodded and then stood waiting for the aunt and niece to leave the area.

'We'll just head down now to Mrs Bridge. I think we'll be spending the night with her, Captain, trying to keep her calm. Probably for the best.'

'Well, thank you for your assistance, and like I say, try to keep your niece under control.'

Tiffany was raging, but Catriona grabbed her hand, squeezing it hard. When she turned her back to the captain, she shot a glance to Tiff that said shut up. As they walked back to the cabin of Mrs Bridge, Tiff was indignant. There were still two guards outside, Scott Jones, and Jack Fogherty. As Cat came up to them, she begged that they would wait for another five minutes while she took the air on the outside deck. Seeing Mr

Hughes had upset her stomach, and she felt she needed a little light air before retiring. First Officer Jones made to follow her out, but Cat turned around and stopped him.

'It's okay, Tiff will accompany me. I just need to make sure she's okay as well.' With that, she reached over, grabbed Tiff by the hand, and dragged her out onto the outer deck.

'What the hell was all that about?' said Tiff. 'I was just about to put my arm down. I was going to see if he was alive.'

'And then what? What if he is alive? We're stood there, and the captain's hand is forced. If something's up here, we don't want to get caught shouting in people's faces. We're nobodies here. They could just dispose of us. I don't know why things are the way they are, but we need to be careful, Tiff.'

'Anyway, he's alive. Didn't you smell something funny when she opened the bag?' said Tiff. Catriona looked out at the dark sea beyond. There were no lights, just stars. She thought she might be standing on one of the most beautiful spots on earth. Why was it at such a time as this?

'Cat, there was no smell. He's dead. You should smell the dead. Especially wrapped up in a bag like that. There was no smell. I doubt he's even staying in that bag. If he was alive, he'd be sweating. As a dead person, he'll still respire. He'll still give off a stink. There's something afoot there.'

'Come closer, Tiff, a minute. Hold me like I'm in need of something.'

'Why? You know I don't do closeness; I don't do holding. I don't do hugs. Hugs are pointless.'

Catriona sighed. It was true that Tiff did not like people to touch her, to be close, but Cat was requiring it at this time because she could see the first officer looking out at them.

'Tiff, I've just told them we need a moment. We need to look like we are in distress. We need to look like we're having to hang onto each other and certainly don't want to be disturbed by anyone. Get over here and hug me.'

Tiff gave a gentle shake of her head. Catriona stepped forward, wrapped her arms around her niece, held her tight, whispering in her ear, 'I think he's alive, too. I wasn't convinced when she didn't show us the wound. If what you're saying is true, then that certainly changes everything. But why fake his own death? How are we going to know for sure? Everything about the man must be kept in that cabin. It's locked. It's a safe place. Nobody knows the code.'

'Do you have to hold me like this? How long is this going to go on? You know I hate it.'

'I'm trying to talk to you and I'm trying to talk to you quietly. When we go back in the cabin, we've got Mrs Bridge there. That's not going to work, Tiff. So shut up about being hugged and listen. We need to get into that cabin, see what else he has, see what other details are there, have a look at that gun properly. Didn't seem to have exploded to me.'

'You know nothing about guns though.'

'But you got a look,' said Cat, 'Did you?'

'No, I was trying to look at the body. Why would I be looking at the gun? I needed to know if he was dead. I needed to know if he was breathing. I should have just punched him, showed it to be set up.'

'No, you shouldn't. Then we would have been forcing their hand. Something's amiss and I think staying with Mrs Bridge is a good idea tonight. I'm not sure the captain trusts us, but I also want to know why someone wanted to kill Fragrance.'

'Maybe she was investigating,' said Tiff. 'Maybe she knows something's wrong.'

'Well, they tried to kill her, so, we have to be careful too. Hug me, you stupid girl, hug me. He's coming over. Try to smile.' Scott Jones approached. Tiff gave a rather abject effort at hugging.

'Are you okay?' asked Scott.

'We're just having a moment,' said Cat. 'It'd be quite good if we could keep having it alone. Tiff doesn't do opening up in front of strangers.'

'All right,' said the first officer, 'I just wanted to make sure you were okay.'

'That's appreciated. Thank you, but Tiff is just not doing that well at the moment. Please, excuse us.' Catriona watched the man walk back to his post outside Mrs Hughes's cabin.

'He suspects something. All the crew are getting close to people, keeping an eye on them. I'm going to have to flirt more with him,' said Cat.

'That's not going to be difficult. You've been doing that since you arrived, anyway.'

'Stop it. Just stop it. How is that important at this time? What we need to know is how we're going to get back into that cabin.'

'Well, I'll just punch in the code,' said Tiff.

'How are you going to punch in the code?'

'I watched the captain do it. It wasn't difficult. That's the thing. Everybody thinks I'm stupid and thick. It's not easy when you're cleverer than everyone. They don't seem to realise it.'

Cat held her niece closely. *No, they don't,* she thought. 'But you don't realise the danger we're in. We'll need to tread very carefully.' She kept Tiff close for another two minutes before walking back to the cabin. Once Tiff was inside, and after Jack

Fogherty had departed back to his own cabin, Scott Jones held Catriona outside.

'I wish I could look after you tonight,' he said 'You need to be careful. I think the captain's upset with you.'

'The captain and me are fine,' said Cat. 'But I like that you're concerned.' She reached up and this time she kissed him properly. 'When we get all this done,' she said, 'maybe then we can enjoy a bit more time together. But for now, go get a night's sleep. It's 3:00 a.m. already.'

Scott Jones took her hands, rubbing them gently before kissing her forehead. As he walked off, Cat felt a sickness in her stomach. What was he? How could he so easily come onto her like that? She needed to see Mr Popov alone. She needed to be in that cabin and discover what was really going on with the body, if indeed it was a body. She needed to talk to Fragrance to understand what she was doing. Why had somebody tried to kill her? The game was afoot, but why did Catriona still feel like she was wondering what game was being played? Opening the cabin door, she stepped inside and smiled at Mrs Bridge.

'I think we all need to go to sleep, don't we? Maybe we can have a chat in the morning.'

# Chapter 11

Catriona slept with her niece that night, back to back on a spare bed in Harriet's room. But Cat did not sleep much. She watched Harriet turning over several times in the night. Every now and again she would sit up with a start, look desperately around her, then see Cat and Tiff in the bed across from her and lie back down. Was it the walking dead man on her mind or had she really lost something? She said nothing was missing, but was she telling the truth? Catriona wasn't sure and, not having known Harriet for very long, she was struggling to gauge the woman. Without a doubt, the woman was scared and seeking someone to lean on. Cat was quite happy to be supportive, but she also wanted to understand what was happening and decided that she needed to talk to Harriet later that morning.

When the time came to get up, Cat and Tiff took turns going back to their room to grab a shower, before returning to Harriet. Mrs Bridge showered in her own room before dressing in track bottoms and a track top and making her way down to the stateroom accompanied by Cat and Tiff. Cat wore a baggy white jumper and jeans trying to stay as relaxed as possible, but inside, her stomach was churning. She had looked out the window from Harriet's cabin that morning and realised just how far away from civilization they were. Everything around them was ice and at the moment Captain Jollye was not heading for any port and when they did get there, what would happen? They would need to land in Canada or Alaska, but so far no one had said where. A thought ran through Cat's mind: *Were they even going to land anywhere? Why would they need to if Ernest weren't actually dead?* The captain knew this if Tiff was correct in her assumption that the body in the bag was not dead.

Catriona pondered these things as she poured herself a cup of coffee. She looked around and spotted a whisky decanter on the far side of the room. Well, it wouldn't hurt, would it? She needed some Dutch courage at the moment. Crossing over, she dropped a large shot into the black coffee. Cat caught Tiff looking at her, and she swore those were accusing eyes. Sitting down beside her niece, she leaned across and whispered, 'I'm not going to get pissed. I'm merely fortifying myself for what goes on today.'

Tiff leaned close to her ear, 'We need to get in that room. If we can get in that room, we can prove that he's not dead. If we do that, we can bring it up in front of everyone.'

Mrs Bridge sat opposite them, staring at a single cup of tea in front of her. Mr Denny brought up what looked like a disgusting green concoction. Cat couldn't decide if this was one of the health drinks so favoured by people who run gyms. Tiff stared at it. When a bowl of fruit arrived chopped up, Mr Denny turned to Cat, asking what she would like.

'Scrambled eggs and toast, please. Not too much either. Possibly a little salmon amongst it. Smoked, of course.' Mr Denny noted and then asked Tiff what she would like. She asked for a bagel. When he replied he had the sesame seed ones or those with raisins in it, Tiff explained that she would like it plain.

'I'm afraid we don't have any plain ones.'

'It's okay then; I'll eat nothing,' said Tiff, quite annoyed.

'Tiff, that's not on, you have to eat something,' said Cat. 'What's wrong with a raisin or sesame seeds in a bagel?'

'I just don't like them, you know that.'

'Can you not make do? There's other more important things here than your breakfast.'

'You know I don't eat those, so I'm not going to.'

'How about a croissant, then?'

'Does it have butter in it? You know I don't take butter.'

Cat rolled her eyes while Mr Denny stood there patiently. 'Mr Denny, could you ask the chef if he could make some croissants, preferably without any butter in them? Tell him I'd be most obliged.' Mr Denny bowed, 'Yes, Contessa.'

'Oh, and Mr Denny, there's no need to bow. I've told you before, I'm not royalty. I'm just like any other guest here.'

'Yes, ma'am,' said Mr Denny, heading off to the galley. Cat could hear a slight cry from the chef who'd obviously been told that he was now to make croissants, but that was what the man was paid for, although maybe she could get down and find out something from him. Mr Popov was rarely about. Maybe this was because he spent most of his time in the galley, but the galley was hard to get to. It was technically off-limits to the guests. Therefore, she would have to see Mr Popov in the crew quarters again, technically off-limits to the guests too, unless invited.

At the side of the stateroom was an itinerary, and today a boat was to be dispatched to see large whales in the area. Cat decided that she didn't want to go on any trip, preferring to stay close to home and see if she could get into the cabin.

'Tiff, you think Captain Jollye will be away? We could sneak in then.'

'Yes, but we'll need to have a reason for staying so no one has to stay here with us. Do you think it would be Popov staying? You quite like him, don't you?'

'I didn't say I liked him. I just don't think he's involved. He warned me.'

When Mr Denny returned with egg and salmon on toast and some croissants, he politely left the women to their food and Catriona realised that they were as alone as they were going to be unless they got back into the room. Maybe this was a time to broach things with Mrs Bridge.

'Harriet, you said you hadn't lost anything last night. Are you sure? Because you didn't sleep well. You kept waking up, looking around. You went back to sleep after each episode, so I didn't want to disturb you. Are you okay?'

Cat watched the woman's hand shake. 'No, I'm not okay. I'm afraid my diary is missing, not my work one, my personal one. Somebody stole my diary from the safe. There are things in there that people shouldn't read, confidences, things between me and Ernest, things I've thought about Ernest. Maybe that's why he came back. Maybe that's why.'

'Enough,' said Tiff, 'It's not about coming back. He's alive. He just never died. It's all a charade.'

'Shush,' said Cat, 'Not so loud. It seems that my niece thinks that Mr Hughes didn't die at all and now, I'm starting to believe her. What was the big deal about you and Mr Hughes, anyway? I don't quite understand. Someone said that he helped you start your business, get it up and running.'

'Ernest did. He put a lot of money in. He backed me, also

mentored me through the early stages. He was the one who insisted that I get out front in the business. I was the one who could be seen and I am the face. The middle-aged woman. The woman who looks so well for her years. It's almost a slur, isn't it? Yes, you look well, but only because you're older. Because we didn't expect you to look as good as you do. It's not really a compliment, is it? You just want somebody to say you look nice. Ernest did that, for a time anyway. Since then, I know he moves on—a man of many women but a charmer all the same.'

'Did you have a falling out at all?'

'No,' said Mrs Bridge, 'never fell out, but he took a hump over a business decision I made. You see, I'm not just there to make money through my clothes. I do believe in this. I believe in looking after women's health. We could have opened them up more, looked to attract a more male clientele, younger set, but I'm not there for the younger set. I'm there for women like me who are struggling, who want to keep in shape, who need that sisterly help. I've seen that in you. That's why I turned to you. I see how you look after your niece.'

Cat saw Tiff roll her eyes. 'Why is it everyone says you look after me? The amount of stuff I have to pull you out of.'

'Not now, Tiff. Now is not the time to make this about you, okay? Sorry, Mrs Bridge, go on.'

'The other thing about Ernest is, he has certain preferences, certain things he likes when he's with a woman. Certainly, that he liked with me. Nothing abusive or anything like that. Just games he likes to play, but games that would ruin his reputation. For a man in his position, it's hard to just let it all go. It was too late when I realised why he liked me. It wasn't for my looks, which would have been shallow, but at my age, somebody liking me for my looks is something not to be thrown away. It wasn't for my business brand or me. It was for my age. He wanted a mother figure. I don't have any kids. I didn't want to be a mother figure. I've never been a mother figure. When I told him that, he struggled.'

'But why would that bring him down? What would he have bothered about for that?' asked Catriona.

'The games he used to like to play, I had to tell him off at times. All some elaborate plot. He filmed them, too. He was a bit of a strange one, but I didn't mind. I got my business, got it up and running, so when we parted, I wasn't bitter. I still came and saw him at times, but not in that way anymore. I was never his mother figure. He resented that. But what could I do about it? And I certainly didn't have any baggage with it. He did good by me. I was sad when he was gone, but to see him in my room scared me and now we're out here, God knows where, not going home soon. What is it they want? Why is my diary gone? Are they protecting his image? They think I have something on him?'

'I don't know, Mrs Bridge,' said Catriona, 'But I'm intending to find out. We're not going anywhere fast and if we don't solve this, I'm worried other things could happen.'

'Yes, well,' said Mrs Bridge, 'just keep an eye out for me as well, just in case any of—'

Suddenly, she clammed up. Catriona looked at the stateroom doors. Tara Limpet was standing there, dressed in her uniform, but with a worried look on her face.

'Excuse me, Contessa, ladies, but have you seen Jack Fogherty anywhere?'

'No, I haven't,' said Cat, 'He hasn't been through here. Where did you see him last?'

'Last night, but I haven't seen him this morning.'

'Why do you want him?' asked Tiff.

'It's private, but I need to find him quite urgently. If you see him, tell him I'm looking for him.'

'Well, he can't have gone far,' said Cat, 'It's not that big a boat; he's sure to be somewhere. Have you checked his cabin?'

'Yes,' said Tara, almost dismissively.

*It was a bit of a stupid question*, thought Cat. 'Is he meant to be on this trip today?'

'I don't know,' said Tara, 'I must look that up. I'm meant to be away, that's why I wanted to find him now before the trip took place. It's only another hour or so.'

'Well, we haven't seen him,' said Cat, 'But if we do, we'll tell him you're looking for him.'

'Thank you very much,' said Tara. And as she went to go, Cat called her back.

'Sorry to bother you, but are there wet suits that we could use. We're just looking to go for a little swim this afternoon. They said it'd be better to stay here than go out on the whale trip.'

'Well, there's scuba gear and things like that. I'm not sure who'll stay with you. Mr Denny is capable of doing that. Popov usually remains on board, though I don't think he's done any scuba diving. Maybe our first officer will. From what I've seen, he's certainly keen on you, anyway.'

*Well, that's a bit forward*, thought Cat. *Not really something to say about your senior in your business. But if that's the feeling around the crew, let's not disappoint them.* Catriona raised her hand up to her neck, fiddling with her ear, almost absent-mindedly looking away. 'Yes, he is quite something. Isn't he? Maybe he would like to scuba this afternoon. If you see him, do mention it.' With that, Tara nodded and disappeared.

'Do you think that's wise?' asked Mrs Bridge.

'Don't worry about me,' said Cat. 'I've had plenty of men try to come onto me before. There's something I want from the first officer, and it's not that. But when I find out what it is, I'll begin to understand a lot better what's going on here.' Cat polished off her scrambled egg with salmon and then looked at the plate beside her. 'Tiff, you haven't had your croissant.'

'It's not right,' said Tiff. 'I'm sure there's butter in here.'

Catriona reached over, pulled a bit off, stuck it in her mouth, chewed it before swallowing it. 'Can't taste any butter in that. Get it down you; otherwise, you won't be strong enough to swim this afternoon. What are you going to do, Mrs Bridge?' asked Catriona. 'Are you going to go off on the excursion?'

'I might do it to take my mind off,' she said. 'But I need to make sure there's someone with me. I think I'll talk to the Professor.'

'Do you know him?'

'Oh yes,' said Mrs Bridge. 'We met before at several parties Ernest held. I think he's okay. He's certainly not on the side of the captain. And like yourself, he could be an ally.'

'Well, just be careful,' said Catriona. 'I'm not sure who to trust at the moment.'

'But you trust me, don't you?' said Mrs Bridge.

'Of course,' said Cat. 'A sister in need is a friend indeed.' She watched Mrs Bridge smile before the three of them stood up from the table. Cat hung back to finish off her coffee, and Tiff waited with her while Mrs Bridge disappeared.

'Do you really trust her?' said Tiff.

'You have to stop taking everything I say so literally.'

'So, you're lying to her?'

'It's not a lie. It's just keeping my options open because at the moment, I'm not sure where to play my cards.'

# Chapter 12

Catriona pulled at the wetsuit. Why are these blasted things always so hard to get on? One leg had taken her five minutes, now the second leg was struggling. She felt ridiculous, stood in her bikini and then pulling the wetsuit on over it. Tiff had had no problems at all. That was the thing about Tiff, she was a thinner person. Catriona was not fat, but she had hips and she had legs that were chunky. Yes, they were toned, but she was no skinny whiff. She was happy with her figure as well and did not see herself as having any excess weight, but what she did have was shape and what wetsuits did not like was shape.

'God, Tiff, give me a hand with this. Bloody hell, how hard do you have to pull these things?'

'Well, mine came on, no problem. Maybe it's the wrong size; maybe it's too small for you.'

'Tiff, I have been a size ten since I got to eighteen. I have not gone over a size ten—I have not made it to a twelve. This wetsuit will fit fine, it's just stubborn.' Tiff reached down and grabbed the leg of Cat's wetsuit. She pulled and made a strenuous sound, as if to emphasise the effort it was taking. Catriona was not amused. 'You can cut that out—just pull the damn thing on for me.'

'Lucky for you, the first officer is joining us and I still don't trust him. I don't think you should either.'

'Tiff, I'm not trusting him, but he is nice. I would like to not put him out if he is kosher. I'd like to think his interest in me is for me.'

'I doubt that,' said Tiff.

'Why? Why do you doubt that? Why can't a man be interested in me?'

'Well, if they are, you're just a widow on the rebound with money. I wouldn't get interested in him. I wouldn't worry about it. It's bound to happen to a woman in your place.'

'Just pull the damn wetsuit on.' It took another five minutes for Cat to get fully into her wetsuit, but when Tiff zipped it up at the back, Cat felt like she'd been clamped in place. But once in the water, she was sure she would feel better. At the moment, she felt like she was strung up. They had seen the trip to watch the whales depart a half hour before, along with Tara Limpet, but still, no one had seen Jack Fogherty.

'What was Fogherty like when you were talking to him?' Cat asked.

'Oh, he was telling me all about engines; he was quite dull, really. I think he felt out of sorts, out of place here; that's why he was talking to me. Probably looked for the person with the brains in the room.'

Cat shook her head again. One thing Tiff didn't lack was confidence in her own superiority. Well, at least not until she had to stand out from the crowd and do things on her own. If it was something she didn't understand or handle, she shied back. That was part of being Tiff and something that Catriona found annoying. Why couldn't she just make a stab at things sometimes instead of shying away?

There were very few remaining with most of the guests and crew going off on the whale-watching trip. In fact, only the first officer and Popov, the chef, remained as far as Cat understood. Someone came and knocked at the door. Cat knew who it would be. Opening it, she saw Scott Jones stood in a wetsuit of his own, smiling broadly. 'You want to go for a swim? Let's go. I can find us some scuba gear if you want.'

'I'll be okay,' said Cat, 'I don't feel like diving deep. I just want to go and have a swim. I'm quite proficient.'

'I saw that the day you went after Ms Paradise. Extraordinarily strong swimmer. You did well that day.' The man sounded impressed, and Cat felt good about that.

Cat let Tiff out of the door before locking the cabin behind her. She then let First Officer Jones escort her down to the aft of the vessel. There was a small, almost ledge-like piece from which people could dive into the water. It was also where the small landing rib came alongside the boat to let the passengers on and off. As they arrived there, Cat was surprised to see someone else. A pair of long, pale legs rose up to a pair of green bikini bottoms and then a green top. It was a half-cut t-shirt which had long blonde hair flowing down behind it. When the figure turned around, she saw the face of Fragrance Paradise.

'I hope you don't mind me joining you for a swim today?' said Fragrance.

'Not at all,' said Scott Jones. Cat caught his look at the woman. *He was escorting me down*, she thought. *You don't upstage me like that.*

'Doesn't she require some sort of wetsuit?' said Cat. 'Probably best if we all cover up going into the water.'

'Well, it's entirely up to Ms Paradise,' said Scott Jones, 'But

I would recommend it. It can be very cold in there, that is, if you're going into the water. You'll be fine to remain like that if you're just going to dip your legs into the back here.'

'Well, I wouldn't want to miss the fun,' said Fragrance.

'Brave of you, though,' said Tiff. 'The last time you were in the water you weren't much good.'

Cat slipped a quick punch into the back of Tiff, 'Shush, that's uncalled for. That was a nasty experience.'

'It's okay,' said Fragrance, 'I know she doesn't mean it.'

'Oh, she means it fully,' said Cat. 'Says what she thinks, this one. Subtle as a brick.'

Tiff shook her head at her aunt before stepping forward and diving off the aft of the boat.

'If you let me get Ms Fragrance a wet suit, I'll join you in just a minute. Please feel free, Contessa, to jump on in.' Cat wasn't ready to jump in. She would rather remain and make sure that First Officer Jones didn't get too close to Ms Paradise. If she needed help into her wet suit, Cat was going to provide it, or even better, she'd get Tiff out of the water to help her. Everyone should endure being put in a wet suit by Tiff. You'll hate the things for the rest of your life, but she could hardly use that defence. So, reluctantly, she dived on into the water, making sure that her dive looked spot on.

The wet suit protected against the cold to a point, but the water was refreshing, and Cat immediately began to swim around. She took it gently at first, letting her body acclimatise before striking out. When she looked back at the boat, she saw Fragrance struggling with her wet suit. A pang of jealously ran through her. Scott Jones seemed to be assisting from awfully close quarters. *I saved her life*, she thought, *the least she could do is lay off the man coming after me, and what's she doing here?*

*Why's she still in the boat? The Professor's on the whale trip. If she seriously thought someone was trying to kill her, why would she stay where there are fewer numbers?*

Catriona swam back over towards the boat and Paradise jumped in. It was not a technically proficient dive; she simply leapt in feet first and then seemed to half cling on to the boat rather than swim around. Scott Jones was not so timid, leaping off the back and almost showing off as he swam back and forward. A shoal of fish passed off to the side, and Cat dived under the water, trying to see as far as she could, but the shoal disappeared quickly. When she came up, she felt the water running off her hair, across her face, but she also saw Fragrance Paradise pulling herself out of the water, sitting on the landing platform at the aft of the boat. Scott Jones was sitting beside her now, unzipping her at the back, and seeing the pair of them were rolling down the top of their wet suits, there was a pang of jealously within Cat. Part of her wanted to swim over, pull herself out of the water, and do exactly the same.

The woman was so brazen. Clearly, she was trying to entice Scott Jones, but why? She had a partner. He was away with the whales. Why was she suddenly here? It wasn't like he had been in distress when he thought she was dead. Cat decided she'd had enough and swam over, pulling herself up alongside Scott Jones. She saw his rippled chest and certainly appreciated it, but she thought he looked a little too smug. The point was she was supposed to keep him entertained, keep him thinking that he was attracting her. Part of him was and Cat was worried that this was a dangerous game she was playing.

'Can you unzip me at the back?' said Cat. Scott pulled down the zipper before pushing the wetsuit off her shoulders and down to her waist, freeing her arms in the process. Cat felt the cold air around her. This was such a bad idea.

'I could almost retire to the Jacuzzi,' said Cat.

'The fresh air not suit you?' said Fragrance. 'I'm quite happy here but please if you want, go on.'

'What do you think, Scott?' asked Cat.

'No, I'm quite happy here, too,' said Scott, 'but don't let me stop you.'

It really was bothering Catriona. *Why am I getting so uptight? It's not like I would have been bothered with him ditching me a week ago. I'm here to investigate and he's got to be a suspect, of what I don't know, but he's probably in on it. And anyway, where's Tiff?* Catriona looked around her and saw no sign of Tiff in the water.

'Tiff! Tiff, where are you? Tiff!' She shouted. She heard no sign. 'Where the hell's she gone? Scott, where's Tiff? Where is Tiff?' Catriona was up on her feet, looking around either side of the boat. 'Where's she got to?'

Scott got up on his feet now as well.

'Maybe I should dive in and try to find her?'

'Don't go anywhere yet,' said Cat, 'She was just off the back of the boat here.'

'She can't have gone far then,' said Fragrance. 'I did see her, not that long ago. You don't think she swam off a bit? Is she a good swimmer?'

'She's good,' said Cat, 'but these waters are cold; she's not used to the open water swimming like me. Tiff! Tiff!' Catriona tied her wetsuit up in front of her and quickly dived in. The cold water grabbed her skin. She cursed herself for not putting on the wetsuit fully, but she was only having a quick look. And then she thought she saw a figure in the distance. It was not that far away because the light penetrated the water so poorly, you couldn't see far but someone, something, was coming towards her. And then that figure was going up, up to the surface, so Cat kicked and swam up as well. As she broke through the water, she saw Tiff in front of her, but beside Tiff's head was another one. Curly ringlets were held tight to a man's head, but she saw that the eyes were not open.

'Give me a hand,' said Tiff, 'He'll be heavy once we get him above the water.'

'What do you mean, get him above the water? Who the hell's this?' But having seen the hair, it dawned on Cat who it was.

'Scott, get something to help us. We're going to need to pull him out of the water.' Scott Jones ran and came back with a large pole with a loop on it, plunging it into the water. He adjusted the pole, so it went around the man's arm, and then pulled him towards the aft of the boat. Paradise reached down with him, and together, they pulled the body of Jack Fogherty onto the aft of the vessel. There was a rope around his legs and a loose one across the arms.

'I think the ropes were attached to some fenders. It was dragged down deep underneath, and I think the fenders escaped. He's gone off over the side at some point,' said Tiff, 'I can't tell if he was pushed or not.'

'Pushed? Let's just hold on a minute,' said Scott, 'What do you mean pushed? The man's obviously fallen in.' Scott's hand was down by the side of Jack Fogherty's neck, 'He's dead, there's no pulse. Dear God, he's dead.' Fragrance looked down at him and Cat was expecting her to scream, but she said not a word. Suddenly behind Jack appeared a figure, and Cat saw the bald head of Mr Popov.

'Popov, get me a body bag from the storage.'

'Do we keep a second one? I didn't think we had more than

one?'

'There'll be one there,' said Scott, 'Go, quick, we don't want this body to be lying here for long.' Scott reached down into the water, pulling Catriona out. She didn't know why, but as she stood on the aft of the boat, she felt the need to put her arms back into the wet suit and have Tiff zip her up. When Popov returned, Scott unzipped the body bag, and together, the five of them placed Jack Fogherty inside of it and closed it up.

'If we all work together, we can carry him. I think it's best if we put him in his room. If no one objects.' They carried the body up the small set of steps and then along the guest quarters before placing the bag on the floor of Jack Fogherty's room.

'Will you stand guard over the cabin, Mr Popov?' asked Scott, 'I need to radio the captain and say what's happened.' Popov nodded. 'Why don't you come with me?' Scott said to Cat, 'I'm sure it's been a shock for all of you ladies.'

'Of course,' said Cat, 'Come on Tiff and Fragrance, we'll follow him,' but as Cat walked off, a hand shot out from the chef grabbing her by the arm, 'Be careful, you can't trust him, you can't trust him at all.'

Cat leaned back, 'Who? Mr Popov,' she said quietly. 'Who?'

'You all right, Cat? Hope Popov isn't scaring you there.'

'I'm fine, I'm fine,' said Cat, 'I'm just coming.' She turned and looked at Popov one more time, but the man was emotionless. Just what the hell did he know?

# Chapter 13

Captain Jollye was not in a good mood when she returned with the rest of the passengers. Hearing of the death of Jack Fogherty, the twenty-seven-year-old racing car driver, the captain decided that she needed to interview everyone to find out about the last movements of Mr Fogherty. In order to do this, she asked that everyone be assigned to their quarters.

Tiff was ignoring the captain completely. Whether it was because she brought the body up that she felt she had a special requirement to be there or that she deserved to investigate herself was unknown, but Cat could see that Tiff was not going to leave the scene without a fight. It took a while for the captain to do this, as the professor was remonstrating with her about what was going on, pointing out again that his partner, Fragrance Paradise's incident, could've been a murder attempt.

'Let's all calm down. Everyone back to your quarters, please. I shall come and speak to you all from there.'

'No way. No, no, no,' said the professor. 'One by one, you come to our quarters? How do we know you're not involved? How do we know this isn't your doing? I think we should stay together.'

'Excellent idea, professor,' said Mrs Bridges. 'We should all stay together in the stateroom. Everyone. That way, we can sit, have a drink. You can take us aside one by one to interview us, but at least, we'll all be together. We'll all be safe.'

'Indeed,' said the professor, 'We'll all be safe. That much you must grant us, Captain.'

Captain Jollye surveyed the scene in front of her. The mood amongst the guests was not good. Cat reckoned she could see which way the wind was blowing. 'Fine,' said Jollye. 'Everyone into the stateroom. Take a seat. Mr Popov, please accommodate our guests with some food. Mr Denny, take care of their needs. Miss Limpet, you're with me. Mr Jones, also with me.'

'Some of us would like to get changed,' said Fragrance Paradise, rubbing her bare arms. Cat wondered why the woman hadn't had the sense to cover herself back up. This was no place to be standing around on deck when you had a perfectly good wetsuit to cover you. Cat was feeling the cold herself and she had covered up, unlike Tiff who seemed to be impervious despite having been the last out of the water.

'Of course, you may return to your cabin, but I'll expect to see you down in the next twenty minutes, Miss Paradise.'

'I shall accompany her upstairs,' said the professor. 'You shall see us in twenty minutes.' The captain spoke to Mr Jones, and then Cat saw Tara Limpet and the first officer make for Fogherty's room. She was going to step over and ask Tiff to remove herself from the situation, but the captain touched Cat on her arm, pulling her aside.

'This is all going to get very heated, and I could do with someone with some sense. Please, can you try to calm them down in the stateroom? It's probably just an accident. The man's fallen overboard, got tied up in some ropes, but I'll need to investigate.'

'Is there any reason why Mr Fogherty and Mr Hughes would both be targeted?' asked Cat. 'From what I gather, they were both involved in the racing team that Mr Fogherty drives for. Is there anything untoward going on there?'

Captain Jollye stepped back. 'I'm asking for calm heads,' she said, 'not for a Miss Marple figure. If you can, please just calm everyone in the stateroom. A woman of your class, your authority, would be much appreciated at this time.'

But Catriona smiled. If only she believed what the captain was saying was true. She did have class. She was a Contessa after all, but she was being softly thrown off the investigation. Cat watched the captain make for Fogherty's room, and when she had grabbed a lungful of fresh air, Cat made for the stateroom. Then a cry came from Tiff.

'Get your hands off him. I'm examining.'

'Hey, Contessa, could you please ask your niece to step back?'

'Cat, come here. Look at this. Can you see? The side of the man's neck. Look at those markings.' Cat ran over, followed by Captain Jollye. There were indeed markings on the side of the neck, but the captain reached forward and gently stroked them.

'Looks like some bruising from when he went in. It's not uncommon; sometimes people hit the rails, the head catches something on the way down. Maybe that's why he didn't surface back up. He was knocked out, couldn't cry for help.'

'He was wrapped up, caught in the ropes,' said Tiff, 'apart from that rope at the bottom.' Everyone looked at the rope around the feet of Jack Fogherty. 'That doesn't come from anything on this boat. That looks like normal rope. I doubt that's even been used on deck.'

'Your niece seems to think she knows a lot about everything, doesn't she?' said the captain sternly.

'It's okay. I'll take her with me,' said Cat. With that, she reached forward, putting a hand on Tiff's shoulder.

'Not now. I am looking at this,' said Tiff.

'We need to go. It would be appropriate at this time to leave before we upset people,' said Catriona.

Tiff turned around, looked up, and rolled her eyes. Catriona saw the anger, but surely, Tiff knew when to trust her, when Cat could read the situation. Tiff had no ability to read people. Cold, hard facts she was good with, but not reading people. It was part of the condition, as they called it. It was just Tiff. 'Come on,' said Catriona, 'back out of the cabin. Off you go.' With that, she pushed Tiff away and watched as the girl sloped off. Catriona turned to walk as well, but a hand grabbed hers and the captain pulled her again to one side. 'Sure, when this is all over, we'll have a laugh about it,' said the captain.

Catriona was struggling to see how this was going to be humorous. 'If you're not feeling good and you need some help, don't be afraid to say.' With that, Captain Jollye reached behind her and untied her hair, and the black mane flew over her shoulders.

*How did people ever get hair to shine like that?* thought Cat. *I have nice ringlets, but they always look greasy.* Then she saw the eyes looking into hers. *Oh, heck,* she thought, *no. If Mr Jones decided his efforts weren't good enough, maybe they reckoned I needed female company.*

'I'll bear that in mind,' said Cat and reached forward, kissing the captain on the cheek. 'Thank you.' She turned and walked away, almost spitting on the floor. *Play the part. Always play the part,* she told herself. *That's where Tiff did it wrong. What were these people so afraid of? Why were they so scared? A bit of investigation.* Entering her cabin, she heard Tiffany shower, and she began to try to undo her own wetsuit. When Tiff emerged wrapped up in a towel, Cat stood with her back to her asking her to unzip.

'You're always chasing me away. See those bruises; they were around the neck. That man was killed. For some reason, he was killed. We need to get back into his cabin.'

'We can't get into his cabin right now. It's daylight; we're meant to be in the stateroom and everyone together. Not the time, Tiff. It doesn't mean we can't do a little investigating of our own when we're downstairs.'

'What do you mean?' asked Tiff.

'Everybody's going to be there with nothing to do. Let's find out what these connections are really about. Let's see who hates who. You see, I think Mr Hughes was searching for something. That's why they're all here. I think the captain's onto it.'

'You don't think she's a captain? You think she's some sort of spy?'

Catriona let Tiff pull down the wetsuit, and she then dragged her legs out of it. 'No. She's a captain all right, but she told me she was close to him. Proper close. As in, in-bed close. She's playing a line for him. I'm sure of it. She just tried to come on to me.' Catriona turned around and she saw Tiff staring up and down at her.

'Why you? If she were going to try that, surely she would have tried it with me.'

Cat shook her head. 'Seriously, that's all you can think of at the moment.' With that, she retired to the shower. When she came out ten minutes later, Tiff was lying on the bed, earphones in. Catriona dressed herself and then grabbed Tiff's hand, insisting they head for the stateroom.

'It's time to get friendly,' said Cat as she entered. 'Move around, talk to people, see what you can do.'

Tiff stared back at her. 'I don't talk to people. You know that. Why would I talk to people?'

'Because we're investigating, you know? You talk to them. You see what they drop into conversation. You read things.' Tiff's face was blank. 'Like when you spoke to Jack Fogherty, did you not get anything from him?'

'How not to drive around the corner,' said Tiff. 'There didn't seem to be a lot he knew. He didn't talk about a lot. It was all racing. Nothing else.'

'Was he interested in you in any way?'

'Not as far as I could tell,' said Tiff. *That was it, wasn't it?* thought Catriona? Not as far as Tiff could tell. In other words, who the heck knew because Tiff wouldn't spot it a mile off. If a man approached her in a pair of budgie smugglers holding a set of flowers, she still wouldn't understand why he was there. Tiff's world must be hugely different to be in.

From behind, Catriona heard someone arrive and turned to see the professor with Fragrance on his arm. Having stood in front of everyone in the bikini, she was now in a short skirt and top that was clearly at home on her figure. *Maybe it was for the professor's benefit. Some men are like that*, thought Cat. There was something else about the woman. Why did she stay behind when she was scared? They tried to kill her, or so she thought. Takes a bit of grit to stay on your own when she hadn't shown herself to be that. If she were simply a money-grabber, she could have just left or at least kicked up in a fuss about it. Get in a helicopter. Get away.

What if she was actually interested in the professor—his dealings with Mr Hughes? Maybe she had a reason to stay. Cat thought it was time to put a bit more pressure on her. Making her way over to the professor and Miss Paradise, Cat asked if either of them would like a drink.

'Oh, I can get that,' said the professor.

'Excellent,' said Cat. 'Leave us girls to have a little chat.' With that, she plonked herself on a seat beside Fragrance.

'It's quite the outfit,' said Cat. 'I haven't got so daring as to wear something like that myself.'

'You should. You've got the figure for it and you've got the title, and that first officer's falling over himself.'

'Are you interested?' said Cat. That was forward, but then she was good at doing forward. 'I saw you today back out of the water—bikinis—felt like a bit of competition.'

She saw Fragrance begin to laugh. 'I have my man,' she said.

'Yet you stayed. How are you feeling after the attack?'

'Okay,' said Fragrance, 'I'm still lucky you were there.'

'How long have you and the professor been together? Because, as much as you're dressed to impress, he doesn't seem that interested in you. To my mind, he's not interested at all. You're not family, are you?' Fragrance looked away, and Catriona knew she hit something. 'Why is the professor here?'

At that moment, the professor himself returned, holding a cocktail for each of the women. Cat smiled up at him, clinked glasses, and then said, 'Do you mind, professor? Girl talk. It's okay. We won't talk about you.' There was nothing in his face. No panic, no worry, nothing. He simply nodded and walked off. *Interesting*, thought Cat.

'Was he surprised by the invitation to come here?' Fragrance tried to hold her face, but Cat saw the telltale reads. The way her lips pursed slightly. The eyes blinked. She was onto something. In her short life, she had learned to hear the real things going on behind what was said and she had taught herself to read people. That was important in the society that she moved in, where people said one thing and meant something entirely different.

'We keep this between ourselves, but yes, he was worried. Things have not been good between Mr Hughes and the professor. Mr Hughes's businesses have some unethical practices and the professor was ready to show them up. Then this invitation came. Heinrich was worried. He called me for my services.'

'Your services?' whispered Cat.

'I work for the professor all the time. Keeping an eye on threats to his businesses, that's why I'm here. As for your first officer, I don't trust him and I don't think you do either.'

'No,' said Cat. 'Why tell me? Why are you going to keep up the pretence?'

'There's not many people I can trust. You're certainly not part of it. You saved me. Your niece brings up a body from the water that was meant to stay under. We need friends when we do this, when we move in the dark. I think you're a friend, and if I were you, I wouldn't get too close to Mr Jones.'

'To be honest, I was just doing one of your tricks, trying to attract him with a little flesh, see what I could find out.' Inside, Catriona knew that wasn't strictly true. Yes, she wanted to know everything the man knew, but there was a part of her that was interested in a more primal way.

'Don't trust him,' said Fragrance. 'Now, if you will excuse me, I need to mingle and find out some other things, starting with Mr Kopeck.'

Cat sat there watching her and realised she was looking at a real pro. Fragrance had that ability to work on a man right in view of everyone. *What if I was making it so obvious?* She watched Mr Kopeck's eyes. She saw him swallow a couple of times. He was nervous, a little giddy by the attention shown to him by Fragrance. *That woman was an operator, and she had learned something interesting. The business between the professor and Mr Hughes was showing up as the professor being in the right, and Mr Hughes was doing things that were unethical. The professor wanted to show everyone. Was he going to deal with it like make a public statement or a show of force, or was the professor doing something subtler?*

*Mrs Bridge knew things that would tend to tarnish Mr Hughes's image. Now, the professor seems to have that in common as well. What did Jack Fogherty know? Tiff was right. They needed to find out. Maybe there was something inside the cabin. Why was Popov warning her? There were a lot of pieces that she couldn't quite put all together.*

Cat needed to see how Tiff was getting on, and she looked over to her niece in the far corner of the room. She was simply standing there. Social situations, the very things that Cat excelled in, Tiff fell apart in. She stood up and went over to her niece to rescue her.

# Chapter 14

'It might be a good idea to at least stand there with a drink,' said Cat to her niece. Tiff was looking up at pictures. The ones that adorned the stateroom. Cat could feel her uncomfortableness. 'It's just talk—just chat about anything. Nothing at all. Then you start finding out things. Try the professor, he can't be that difficult, and Mr Kopeck, oh, I think I want a word with him. Sarah Godwin might talk to you. After all, you're the niece of a Contessa.' Tiff raised her eyes. 'Okay, I'll get Bridge then.'

'Well, we know about Mrs Bridge, diary missing. Knew things about Mr Hughes that the rest of the world didn't want to know.'

'Guess what? So does the professor. Whatever company he's working with—Mr Hughes—it appears that he knows something unethical about him.'

'So, the man was open to blackmail?' said Tiff. 'It starts to make more sense.' Cat was not sure just how much sense it made so she lifted her eyebrows indicating she wanted to know more. 'Can't you see it?' said Tiff. 'I mean, it's pretty obvious. If he's getting blackmailed, he's going to want to bring potential blackmailers here and find out about them. Bring them onto the boat, pretend he's dead, walk around, find out stuff. Anybody sees anything then "Oh, it's the ghost of so and so." No one's going to believe them. Just an outbreak of hysterics.'

'What about Mr Fogherty then? How does he work? He is dead.'

Tiff looked up at the photos again on the wall of the stateroom. 'I know,' she said 'And I think I know why. He always seemed noticeably quiet, Jack, and safe, but from the little conversation I had with him, he was intense whenever he was on about issues that he honestly believed in. I think he must have known something, and he must have been ready to expose Mr Hughes. Especially with him dead. He said he was a close friend of Hughes, so he knew something. After the man was dead, it was the time to bring it out. It couldn't hurt him anymore, but I don't know what it was.'

'How do you know he was close to him? I thought that all you two talked about were cars and racing. How not to go around corners and crash. You're not Sherlock Holmes. You have to convince me a little more than that.'

'Hmm,' said Tiff, 'Everything's in front of your eyes, and you don't even look. All the photographs in the stateroom, I would say 60% to 70% racing cars. Of those, 90%, Mr Hughes, Jack Fogherty. Everybody else in this trip, not on the wall. I think Mr Fogherty was more than just a business partner or somebody he knew. He was a close buddy. Good friend for somebody that powerful. Someone who didn't speak out of turn. Not someone like you who throws the liquor down your throat and can say anything.'

'Yet, he suspected him,' whispered Cat.

'Of course, Tara Limpet in Fogherty's room. Maybe she was sent to probe him like they're sending that first officer after you.'

'Stop it. I think Mr Jones is doing more than trying to get information from me. Sometimes men are just attracted.'

Tiff rolled her eyes. 'If you want to believe these things, you can believe them. I, however, need to get on the move. Do you think you can cover for me while I try to get into the cabin of Jack Fogherty?'

*Cover?* thought Cat. *People would be more likely to miss the plant in the corner.* 'Don't be too long, just in case Jollye starts asking questions. That's her coming into the room now.'

Captain Jollye was indeed marching into the room. Her long hair not tied up but hanging around her shoulders, setting off the crisp white blouse she was wearing. 'Right, everyone. I'm prepared to start doing my investigations. I'll bring you in one at a time to the room just outside the stateroom here. You can, of course, have someone accompany you if you wish. I want everyone to at least feel comfortable while we go through what has happened. Maybe we could start with yourself, professor.'

The professor nodded and Fragrance stepped up to his side. 'Do you want me to come with you, dear?' she said. The man shook his head and then followed Captain Jollye outside. First Officer Jones, Tara Limpet, and Mr Denny entered the room. Mr Popov also attended via the door down to the galley. 'I can see everyone's here,' said the first officer. 'Please have a drink, enjoy yourself. Mr Popov will attend to any food requirements you have and let's just let the captain do her work.'

The stateroom door was open, but the first officer was standing close by it. 'Watch me.' Cat said to Tiff. 'And then when you get your chance, off you go, but don't be long. If Jollye comes back asking for you and you're not here, we'll be in trouble.'

She watched her niece nod, and Cat turned to walk across to First Officer Jones. She was wearing her jeans and the large cream jumper, but for what she wanted to do now, she needed to strike a pose. Pulling the jumper off up and over her head, she set it down on a chair at the side. She was wearing a crop top underneath, mainly as an extra layer to help keep her body warm. She really had given no thoughts of what it looked like. To her, it was simply practical, but she reckoned with the bra strap poking out behind that it maybe was something else to the first officer. Almost strutting over, she made sure she was in full view of him and came up close, placing her hand on his. Gently, she spun in front of him, turning his back to the door. 'Warm in here, isn't it?' she said and watched as her niece passed behind them and out of the door.

Created with Sketch.

Tiff was in her element, away from all the stupid talking, people pretending to be this and that. She was off and actually investigating. As she came up to the guest cabins, it was not difficult to walk along quietly. Tiff's light frame allowed her to creep without making a lot of noise. When she reached the cabin, she pulled a pair of gloves out and looked at the keypad in front of her. She hadn't told her aunt that she'd been brought back by Mr Fogherty. She preferred to keep that to herself because her aunt would've thought that he'd been up to something, when in fact, all that Mr Fogherty wanted to do was to show her the schematics of the engine he was driving.

Cat would've probably assumed the man was gay. What was it with people these days, always trying to guess orientations? Who cares what people are? The man was interested in motors, and to be fair, he was more interesting than a lot of other people here, but Tiff had remembered the code for the room.

It was natural to her to see things—numbers, patterns—and just implant them in her mind.

Pushing the door open and then closing it gently behind her, she looked again in the room she'd been in previously. The black bag was lying on the bed. Carefully walking up to it, she pulled down the zip and saw the deceased Jack Fogherty. Her hand went forward looking for a pulse and found none. The man was cold.

As she unzipped further, she saw his skin was white. Tiff checked his hands to see if anything was there, and then his feet, and the rest of his body before zipping it back up again. There was nothing. They had stripped him clean. She took to walking around the drawers, pulling one open after another. Tiff found most were empty, but two of them had large files within them. When she opened the files, she saw schematics for engines and there were charts about pressures and various other car components. Everything said Jack Fogherty about it. The man seemed to live cars and nothing else.

Then she saw a smaller file. It was leather bound, and Tiff opened it. A picture fell out from inside. It was Tara Limpet. She was in a pair of bikini bottoms and t-shirt on a sandy beach. The woman was smiling.

Tiff turned another couple of pages and found more photographs of her. Then she found letters. They were signed, Tara. Tiff tried to scan them quickly. Most were letters of love and Tiff read through them quickly unbothered, but then there was a discussion about important things. A funding having been withdrawn from the team. Apparently, there had been a crash. Tara reported that within the organisation, it was seen that Mr Hughes had been the one to push forward for a modification without backing it up with a sufficient spend to make it safe. Jack's co-driver, the one who drove with him on the team, had apparently perished. Tara went on to say how much Jack must have missed his friend.

There was so much information in these letters, and Tiff had so little time that she took some of them and started stuffing them inside her pockets. Tiff looked at her watch and realised that she'd been away for over ten minutes. She needed to return and make sure the coast was clear. Locking up the cabin again, she made her way back into the stateroom. Her aunt had been right, no one had noticed her. When she went to grab a drink, soft, of course, she was then able to glide back out with no one being the wiser. Her aunt was almost offering herself in front of that first officer. *She really needs to pick her men better*, thought Tiff. The man was positively all over her.

When back in the cabin, Tiff started searching more drawers with little success. Most things were bare. Just before she would leave again, Tiff decided to do a quick scan around the bed to see if anything was hidden under the sheets. Running her hands through them and around the body in the bag, she felt something as she pressed down on the mattress, but it was underneath.

Reaching down, she felt something metallic. Tiff took it out and found a gun in her hand. Maybe Jack Fogherty was here with another mission. The idea grew in her mind that he had been betrayed, but certainly there were a lot of people who could bribe Mr Hughes. Maybe he was bringing them here to sort it out. What was the point in the Contessa being here, her aunt and herself? They could have simply refused and said there was no room. Maybe they needed somebody genuine. Somebody not linked.

Tiff began to muse. Bit by bit, she saw plans afoot. She would need to talk to her aunt. She would need to think through what was going on. She looked down at her watch. 'Damn.' She'd been thinking too hard. Twenty minutes were gone. Tiff began to run down the stairs. When she turned round towards the stateroom, she heard Captain Jollye come out. Mrs Bridge was with her and had a foul look on her face. Tiff simply waited for the pair to enter the room, then heard the call.

'Contessa, would you be so good to accompany me here? And bring that niece of you with you. Where is she anyway? I can't see your niece.' Tiff quietly walked in behind Captain Jollye. Tapping her on the shoulder, the woman spun around, almost jumping in the process. 'Just in the corner,' said Tiff, 'always in the corner. Shall we?'

# Chapter 15

Catriona and Tiff stepped into the side room along from the stateroom where Captain Jollye was to interview them. There were two seats in front of a small table and a single one behind. Cat heard the door close behind her.

'Well, really, I have to make a scene of this,' the captain said as she manoeuvred her way around the tight space to the seat in front. 'It's not easy doing all of this. Well, at least I know with you two I haven't got something untoward on my hands. All I want from you is Tiff to explain what happened, what you saw, what you found. Exactly how it all came together.'

Tiff sat there, staring straight forward. 'I don't know,' she said. 'Just sort of did.' Cat sighed. When faced with a head-on situation, someone who Tiff clearly suspected in front of her and who she wanted to confront, Tiff struggled. Tiff was scared, yet all she had to do was simply recount what she'd found.

'Come now,' said the captain, 'there's no need to be afraid. No one blames you for Mr Fogherty's death. You simply found him. You stayed behind to go swimming with your aunt and what? Did you see him? Did you see him floating in the water? What happened?'

'Tiff, just answer the captain, please. Just tell her what happened.'

'I was just swimming under the boat. He was there,' said Tiff.

'Was he caught up in all the lines? Is that what it was? Is that why he was held to the ship?'

'Possibly,' said Tiff. 'It was very dark, but you couldn't have mistaken it was a person, and up against the hull. I pulled, and it came loose, but his feet stayed tied because his feet were tied differently.'

'You're suggesting someone tied his feet up,' said the captain, 'But his hands weren't tied. That would be a bit silly.' Tiff raised her eyes and stared at the captain. 'There, you see, obviously, his feet just got caught up by accident. Tragic overboard accident. He must have been out looking at the sky or something, slipped over and gone. It's tragic, especially in the wake of Mr Hughes's accident.'

'At least Mr Hughes didn't die,' said Tiff.

'Will you stop this?' said the captain. 'Contessa, Catriona, can you tell her to stop?'

'The hands were behind the back,' said Tiff. 'There was no rope, but the rigor mortis was setting in and the hands were behind the back.'

A silence filled the room and Cat wondered what to do about it. Better for Tiff to have held her tongue, not to be so forward, especially with someone they didn't trust, but all she stated was a fact and other people had seen this too. They just hadn't got why it was important. Tiff, seeing everything in her own world and her own light, automatically picked up on the warning signs.

'I'll have to check that,' said Captain Jollye. 'Go back up to his room and have a look. Maybe it could have been from other things. Who knows? Thank you for that. He was definitely dead when we brought him up onto the deck.'

'Totally,' said Cat, 'even I could tell that.' Her niece, pressing her knees, flashed eyes at her and Cat felt the rebuke. Fogherty was dead. Surely, she could at least have given her that.

'Was he feeling low at all?' asked the captain. 'He didn't seem depressed at all, did he?'

'No,' said Cat. 'In fact, I thought he was having a good time. I actually saw Tara, your deckhand, and him disappear into his cabin. They seemed to be getting on very well. Tiff spoke to him as well,' said Catriona, spotting the captain swallowing hard before listening again. 'You didn't notice anything, Tiff, when you were with him?'

'No,' said Tiff. 'The man was on motorcars. That's all he spoke about, but he knew his engines. Do you know your engines, Captain?'

'I know the engines of this ship, Miss Munroe. Have you seen anything else around him, Contessa?' asked the captain.

'No,' said Cat. 'Nothing at all. The man didn't say much. Kept himself to himself. Not really as flamboyant as me. Tiff would probably understand him better, and Tiff seemed to think he was fine.'

'Well, thank you,' said the captain standing up. 'Apologies for having to bring you in like this. Please, if you'd return to the stateroom, I think we'll have some lunch, and then afterwards we shall resume our interviews.'

Tiff led the way out into the stateroom. As Cat was about to follow, she felt her hand being grabbed again.

'I mean what I say, Contessa. Oh, sorry. Catriona. If you need anything, just ask. It's not easy at the top. I could do with a good friend like yourself.' Cat nodded, turned around, and gave the captain a hug. It was friendly. Nothing more. As she backed away, Cat winked, 'You're doing very well, Louise. That uniform, it really suits you.' Cat cast her eyes up and down, and she saw Louise smile. Turning away, she grinned. *Things you have to do for an investigation*, she thought. *Louise, you've been laughing at me.*

Returning to the stateroom, Catriona found everyone seated and Mr Popov beginning to serve lunch. There was quiet around the table as soup was had, followed by a light fish salad, after which the captain stood up and announced that the interviews would continue in five minutes' time and she looked over to Tyrrell Kopeck. 'I'm also suggesting,' said the captain, 'that after I conclude my investigations, we confine ourselves to certain areas of the boat, keeping each other well within sight. A quiet night tonight. You are, of course, welcome to use the stateroom. Keep to the aft of the ship, or simply just stay within your cabins, but please don't bother the officers. Keep away from the owner's area and our own area as the crew, and don't go around singly. I'm taking this course of action, not because I feel there's a threat, but because I think it will keep everyone much more reassured.'

That's where Tiff said something under her breath, possibly an expletive, but she knew what she meant. While Cat smiled at the captain, nodding in an encouraging way, she didn't trust the woman at all. Had she put people up for her crew to investigate others? Excusing herself from the stateroom, Cat took Tiff to one side and began to ask about what she had found in the cabin upstairs. Tiff said she had letters in her pocket, but couldn't show them and explained the relationship between Tara and Fogherty. As she did so, Cat caught the eye of First Officer Jones and wondered if she'd been playing him wrong. Maybe the crew weren't being sent to butter up the guests. Tara wasn't; she'd obviously known Fogherty before. Maybe it wasn't the crew that Popov was talking about. Maybe it was the guests. As she pondered this, First Officer Jones came over and asked for a moment of Contessa's time.

'Sorry to take you away from your niece, but it's obviously an unsettling moment. If you wish I can stick around, stay close, just in case you feel anxious at all.' His hand moved quietly to touch Cat's, and she looked up into the man's dark eyes. There was something there. There was a spark. She felt something, but she was also wary. Now is not a time to let anyone in. There was only one person to trust, and that was Tiff.

'It's up to yourself, but I thought Tiff and I would spend some time out on deck this afternoon. A bit of fresh air for the constitution. Tiff had a bit of shock this morning. I know she doesn't show it, but deep inside, she will be shocked.' This was a complete lie, of course. Tiff was thoroughly enjoying the fact she'd found a dead body and seemed to be showing no remorse that it was Fogherty. Sometimes Tiff's world scared Cat.

'I shall do my best to be out there depending on what the captain has for us,' said Mr Scott. 'But remember, if you don't feel safe at any time, I am here and I will protect you, Contessa.'

'As I'm sure you would the entire crew.'

'Of course, but not as closely.'

Cat watched the man disappear out of the stateroom. Something inside her sparked. Was he looking after her? Was he something else? *Heck of a time to take a chance,* she thought.

It turned out that a number of the guests decided that the best thing to do was to stick together, and the rear deck of the vessel was busy that afternoon. Cat lay down on the recliner, wrapped up with a blanket around her. The air was cold and the view stunning, but she didn't feel the need to partake of the jacuzzi. Mrs Gosling was in the jacuzzi and staring hard at Tyrrell Kopeck, who seemed to be heavily occupied talking to Mrs Bridge. Demi Forsyth, who, so far, seemed to pay little attention to the guests, was also in the jacuzzi.

The crew were not around, and many of the guests seemed nervous. Professor Weber approached from his cabin and made his way directly to Cat. Tiff was behind her, leaning on the railings. The professor made no attempt to contact her, instead crouching down and proffering a hand to Catriona. Shaking it, he said, 'I believe we may be friends, so I'd ask that you take special care to look out for us. We're in our cabin at this time, but I thought we might need to stick together.'

'Indeed, a wise manoeuvre,' said Catriona. 'But I've also got Mrs Bridge to look after, and she's on her own. From what Fragrance told me earlier, she may be able to handle herself.'

'Very much so, except she is still very raw at this game. I have lost people before in my line of work,' said the professor.

'And what line of work is that?'

'I'm a chemical expert,' said the professor. 'And most people think that what I do is not dangerous, but I make the stuff that they use in the services around the world. The ones that put people to sleep. The ones that remove people. That's the company where the money of Mr Hughes was, and quite frankly, he was starting to sell it to some rather unsavoury characters. I was going to confront him with it, this trip. Maybe that's why he wanted me here. Still, Fragrance is good, but she's not infallible. I'd hate to see something happen to her.'

'And she'd hate to see something happen to you, sir.'

'Indeed, but be wary.'

'You're not the first person to say that to me,' said Catriona.

Suddenly, Sarah Gosling stood up from the jacuzzi. 'How about we all go off the back for a swim, hey? Let's all get changed. We need to liven this up. What could happen when everybody's together? Let's all get our costumes on and let's all jump in the water. Liven this up a bit. What do you say?'

'Well,' said Mrs Bridge, 'that's a bit over the top, is it not?'

'Nonsense. Stop being such a stick in the mud. We need to enjoy ourselves. Just because there's been a couple of accidents. Tyrrell, go and get your bottoms on.' Cat saw Mr Kopeck raise his eyes, but he obediently made his way off. That's the trouble with being a paid man—sometimes you had to toe the line.

'An excellent idea,' said the professor, and then bent back down to Cat. 'Safety in numbers. Safety in numbers.' With that, he marched off, following Tyrrell Kopeck.

Demi Forsyth was still in the jacuzzi and was happily urging people to come and join her. Mrs Bridge looked at Cat, and when Cat nodded back, the woman left for the cabin with Cat and Tiff in tow. As they reached the corridor, she heard a scream that was coming from the guest cabins ahead. Running forward, Cat saw the professor lying on the floor. There was blood coming from the back of his head, but she heard more screaming. It was from the professor's cabin and the door was not fully closed. Opening it up, she saw Fragrance lying on the floor, her face covered in blood. Cat knelt down, placing her ear to the woman's mouth to hear if she was breathing.

'I think she's out cold. What do I do? What do I do?' From behind, a hand went onto her shoulder and almost pushed her aside.

'I've got it under control,' said Tiff. 'Get everybody out. I've got it.'

Cat turned around and saw Mrs Bridge trying to enter. 'Stay back. Stay back. Tiff is dealing with the situation. It's all okay.' There was commotion out in the hallway, and Cat saw First Officer Jones arriving in his crisp white shirt and then kneeling before the professor. Within a minute, some blood had smeared onto his shirt as he got close to make sure the professor was breathing okay. Many of the others had returned from their cabins, now dressed in their swimwear, and it seemed rather bizarre. There was fear and confusion and a lot of cold people standing in the corridor.

'She's going to be all right,' said Tiff. 'I've got her, and she's going to lie on the bed.' Cat saw Captain Jollye racing forward. She pushed her way through the crowd and then into the cabin of the professor. 'I've got her, captain,' said Tiff. 'I know what I'm doing.' Cat followed the captain, and she saw Fragrance open her eyes wide, looking around.

'Didn't see him,' she said. 'Didn't see him.'

'Are you okay?' asked the captain.

'Yes. Where's Heinrich?'

'He's taken a blow,' said Cat. 'First Officer Jones is with him, but I think he's okay.' The captain clapped her hands, 'Everyone, back to your cabins. Everyone, inside your cabins for the next twenty minutes, until we sort this out.'

Mrs Gosling was standing half wet from being in the jacuzzi. 'Do we not get a break from any of this?' she said to the captain. 'Do you know how much we've paid to be here?' The captain rounded on her, hands on hips.

'Show a bit of class. You should be more like the Contessa here.' Cat saw it, the dividing tactics, and she trusted the woman even less. Without waiting for anything further, she made her way back into the cabin and looked at Paradise.

'I didn't see him.'

'How do you know it was a man?' asked Tiff. 'Could have been anyone.'

'I didn't see them,' said Fragrance.

'Has anything been taken?' said Cat, looking around. A few of the drawers were open, and Tiff helped Fragrance to her feet. Slowly, she walked over, looking inside.

'I don't know what it is, but something's missing. Heinrich had a file here. That's the file he wanted to talk to Mr Hughes about.'

# Chapter 16

Having made sure that Fragrance Paradise was okay, Tiff made her way to examine Heinrich. She made no effort to explain why she was the most qualified, instead, just assumed that everybody else would know. Cat was taken aback by Tiff at times. For the girl who was so shy to talk in company, when she got in her head that she was the person to do something, neither hell nor high water could stop her. Even Captain Jollye was brushed aside, and it was only when Tiff gave her the all-clear for the casualties that the captain was able to usher everyone properly back to their rooms.

Once inside, Catriona locked the door and looked at her niece, now lying on the bed, headphones in. She reached over and pulled the blasted devices from her ears.

'What do you think, Tiff?' said Cat. 'What do you think about it all, now there's been something taken from the professors as well?'

'I actually was listening to that.'

'What do you mean listening? We're in the middle of a case here. We're in the middle of an investigation.'

'Case, oh. So now we are Sherlock Holmes? Now we are acting on this? One minute you're telling me to keep clear, and then the next minute we're getting involved and you're asking me questions.'

'I'm doing that because we're in front of people. When we're in front of people, I need us to act like we know nothing, but we need to get to the bottom of this. At the end of the day, according to you, Jack Fogherty was murdered. You said his feet were tied.'

'And his hands,' said Tiff. 'She didn't like it when I made that comment about the rigor mortis, but I'm right. Pretty obvious, really. Wonder what they have to do to become a master of a vessel. That's the word, not captain. You're all calling her captain, but she's the master. That's what the word is in the maritime community. You get a masters' ticket. You don't get a captain's ticket. Certainly, it doesn't seem to have anything to do with investigations.'

'Of course, it doesn't have anything to do with investigation,' said Cat, 'but come on, think about it. What's going on?'

'Well, it's pretty obvious, isn't it? I mean, if we think about it, it's pretty obvious.'

Tiff got like this. She spoke as if everyone followed her train of thought, as if everyone's brain worked in this way. It was always the same. You had to adjust to Tiff. Tiff made no adjustment to you. Maybe that's what it was called, being on the spectrum. Maybe that's how it worked. *For those of us who are not on the spectrum,* thought Catriona, *it's pretty damned annoying.*

'Enlighten me. Tell me about it. Tell it to me straight?'

'Well,' said Tiff, 'if they're looking to see what secrets were held—I mean, they're taking diaries, aren't they? They're taking intimate stuff, things where you might record stuff. In that case, they're probably wondering what they know about them, and also what they're going to do about it. I reckon Jack Fogherty was going to do something. After all, there was a gun under his bed.'

'Well, of course, he was going to do something,' said Cat, 'He had a gun. But what about everyone else? This Harriett Bridge. Is she going to do something? Speaking of which, why is she not in here with us? I thought she wanted company.'

'Going with the professor?' said Tiff. 'I did not see that. I think she reckons that the professor's a target, and certainly Fragrance is, therefore, they can't be doing the killing. Not that stupid, Mrs Bridge wants to get on the correct side. I can understand that. Not sure she is on the right side yet.'

'What do you mean? How is she not on the right side?'

'Fragrance Paradise, Cat, have you not seen? Look at the way she moves about?'

'Yes,' says Cat, 'She's working for Professor Heinrich. She protects him.'

'You never told me that.'

'Well, you need to start listening up. You go out, you make your own decisions, and you stick those blasted earphones in. You need to talk to me, communicate. That's what it's about. You and me operating as if we don't know anything, and then we talk to each other.'

'So, you can give me the information,' said Tiff, 'and I can work out what's going on?'

Catriona shook her head. 'So we can discuss it; so we can come to a conclusion.'

'Well, if you want to be part of the team—' said Tiff.

Catriona had had enough. She was not going to be stuck in the room until morning. And then there came a knock at the door. Cat was wearing a pair of jeans and a slack t-shirt, thinking that she'd be in her room for the rest of the night. At the knock on the door, she instantly looked at the mirror. *What's my hair doing? Is it all right?* she thought and instantly grabbed the brush.

'You're not answering that,' said Cat. Tiff turned and looked at her. 'You should be presentable when you do anything like this. There're no excuses. You never know who's going to be there.'

'Don't trust him.'

'But I need to play my part,' said Cat. *And besides,* she thought, *if he's not on the wrong side, I don't want to put him off.* A minute later and after the door had been knocked twice more, Cat opened it and stood face to face with First Officer Scott Jones.

'Sorry to bother you,' he said 'I was just thinking, wondering how you were. Maybe you could do with a bit of company for a while. We could take a walk around to the deck. You can still see the cabin from here, and then maybe we can have a chat. I'm sure things have been quite upsetting for you.'

Cat smiled. 'Just a moment,' she said. 'I'll just get my shawl.' With that, she headed to the wardrobe. Scott Jones looked over at Tiff, who had her earphones in. 'Quite the woman of the hour you are,' he shouted. Tiff pulled her ears out and gave a questioning look. 'I said you were quite the woman of the hour.'

'You think someone around here would know first aid, wouldn't you?' With that, Tiff put her earphones back on. Cat heard the conversation and almost shuddered as she put her shawl on before turning back to the door and ushering Scott Jones away to the open deck.

'Sorry about that. That's just Tiff. Really, I just don't know what to say about her.'

'If we're not getting used to her by now, we'll never get used to her,' said the first officer, 'but how are you coping? It's quite something to see a dead man hauled up like that.'

'It's worse for Tiff. She brought him up.'

'But she didn't seem that bothered,' said Mr Jones. 'I guess that's the being-on-the-spectrum again.'

'You don't have to talk like it's some sort of disease. It's just the way she is. She's very gifted, very clever. Cleverer than me.'

'But she doesn't quite have your figure, does she?' As they strolled out onto the deck, Cat felt a hand moving down her back. She was unsure where it was going at first until it managed to work its way under her shawl, rubbing up her back. Standing at the ship's railings, the first officer drew Cat close to him.

'It's cold out here. We might want to stay nice and tight.' With that, his other arm wrapped around her.

Cat was unsure what to do. Ideally, she wanted him to stay well clear until everything was done. No, she didn't. *Come on, Cat. You know what you want.* It was one of the things that Luigi liked about her, that she was forthright in her relationships, saying what she wanted when she wanted it, but when she'd been with Luigi, nobody had been dead. No bodies were being washed up, and it was just a lot of fun, usually on the Italian Riviera. Now, she was too far north, too far from anywhere called civilization. She had to trust her instincts more than let them go.

'I'm sorry, Scott. I'm just a little off tonight.' And with that, she moved his hand away and turned round, gripping the rail.

'It's understandable. It can't be easy when your niece keeps saying that. First, they die, then they're still walking around.

Do you find that embarrassing?'

Cat turned and looked up at him. 'I'm never embarrassed by death. Shocked, horrified, not embarrassed. And maybe she's right.'

'Maybe she is. It's another reason I wanted you out here, not purely for company, but I needed to talk to someone,' said the first officer. 'I've not been with Captain Jollye that long, but I know that herself and Mr Hughes were close, but he also had a lot of enemies, people who would ruin his portfolio as he put it. From what I gather, he liked to keep them close, so his enemies may be here. Did you have any dealings with him before you came?'

'No,' said the Contessa. 'I barely knew the man. In fact, I didn't know the man. I think it's my late husband's family. Luigi's family is quite extensive. I don't know where all their money goes. I Just know they have plenty of it, and I've got my hands in it, which is why I'm leading this ridiculous lifestyle.'

'It doesn't seem so ridiculous to me. A woman of your beauty should be able to run where she wants to be admired.'

'Stop right there. Like I said, I don't want anything until we can get sorted. But you were saying you had your concerns about the captain. She seems very proficient to me.'

'But she also seems to be coming close to you. Has she made her move?' asked the first officer.

'A move? You mean like a sexual move, like in actually wanting me for that sort-of-thing move?' Sometimes in her life, Catriona wished she could speak more eloquently. She might be mistaken for royalty, but she certainly could never live up to the bill.

'That's totally what I'm talking about,' said the first officer. 'I think she might try to get close to you to see what you know.'

'But I know nothing.'

'But you are investigating, and Tiff keeps calling her out. Tiff keeps saying this man is walking. What if he is? What will Tiff do if she finds it out to be true? What will you do? Will you contact someone?'

'We have a dead man on our hands now. We should do the right thing, don't you think, Scott?' Cat looked up at the man's eyes, but he was staring out across the sea.

'To do the right thing would not be easy, how to contact people without the captain knowing. It's not like we're sitting off the coast of England or of America, Ireland, or Europe, and you just pick up your mobile and give them a ring. All the contacts at the moment would go through the ship. The captain would see them. She would know.'

'Do you think we should act?' asked Catriona. 'Do you think we've got enough?' She removed her hands from her shoulder and put them on the first officer's. 'Are you convinced that something's wrong? The captain said that Jack Fogherty fell overboard. I'm not convinced, but I have no evidence. I have nothing to say that something was wrong.' Catriona knew this was a lie, but she wanted to see where the first officer was coming from.

'It's hard to do. I think the best thing is I stay close to you, keep an eye on you. Worst comes to worse, we can jump in the rib and leave, head off and find somewhere, another vessel to get on to. Be ready to go in an instant along with your niece. I know you're worried, but you can trust me, Catriona. I'm one of the good guys here. You can trust me. I want to know what's happening as well. It's not going to look good on me if the captain's covering up a murder,' the first officer pointed out.

'Well, we've been into the cabin. We've seen the body, or at least a body. I don't even know what Ernest looked like,' said Catriona. 'Who knows if he was in that bag? Maybe you should take a look.' Cat looked up at the man.

'Don't be ridiculous. How can I get in? We've already been in with the captain.'

'Dead of night. Maybe that's the time to do something.'

"Maybe it is, Cat. There's only one of the crew on watch, and it will be to me later tonight,' said Scott.

'Do you know the code to get in?'

'No. That is a private code not known to the first officer.'

'Well, then we have another problem,' said Cat. 'Maybe I will sniff around tonight, see what I can find.'

'I'll come with you,' said Scott.

'No. You need to be where you need to be. Here, we can say we're being romantic. Here you can say, "Look, I'm taking care of a guest." In the middle of the night, in the cabins you're not meant to be in, we'll both be caught. If Tiff's right, who knows what they could do to us? No. We need to keep it cool.'

'You're quite an impressive woman, aren't you? I mean, what age are you? Oh, look at me. That's silly, isn't it, asking a woman's age? You've got the maturity of a forty-year-old with a body of someone much, much younger.'

'You are very forward and very cheeky. If you think it's getting you anywhere tonight, you're wrong. Kindly escort me back to my cabin.' The first officer nodded and held out his arm, which Catriona took hold of. Together, they walked back the short distance to the cabin. When Catriona knocked, awaiting Tiff to open the door, the first officer grabbed Cat and made a kiss on her lips. When he finished, she stood there looking at him.

'I apologise but I just had to.  You understand that, don't you?' Cat nodded and stepped back inside the cabin, closing the door with her eyes still fixed on the man.

'What sort of sleazeball line was that?' said Tiff in a whisper that could have been heard on the far side of the world.

'I don't know,' said Cat quietly.  'I don't know what he's interested in me for, but we're going to find out, and I think we're going to find out soon.'

# Chapter 17

Cat lay in her bed staring at the ceiling, unable to sleep. Part of her was unsure about Scott Jones, but with the revelation he gave that night about his suspicions around Captain Jollye, she was unsure if she should trust him, or if maybe he was the key to solving everything. He would have access. He would be able to use the ship's devices to contact the authorities. As first officer, he could also relieve the captain if necessary as well as handle the vessel. Everything would be so much easier if he were on her side, but it was a calculation, one she was unsure of.

She had asked Tiff when she'd come back what she thought of him, but the girl was dismissive. It wasn't jealousy, but Cat had learned that Tiff had very fixed opinions at times. There was no definite evidence that Scott was on the wrong side of this. There was a lot of circumstance, but there was a lot of circumstance around everyone. Cat needed to get inside that cabin, the personal one of Ernest Hughes and root around further. Maybe the answers were in there. Would Captain Jollye have left stuff in her own cabin? Surely not. People could gain access. Even just stumbling in to say that they were looking for her. Ernest Hughes's cabin was locked. It was where a dead body was lying, but they had the code.

The other thing that surprised Cat was that Tiff had seemed uninterested in going to the cabin that night since Scott had left her. They had a small discussion, but Tiff refused to take her earphones out. She'd simply lie on the bed listening to whatever music was taking her fancy that day. This frustrated Cat, but it wasn't unusual. Tiff had a habit of changing her mind, and anyway, as she saw it, she'd solved the case. Ernest wasn't dead. In fact, Fogherty had the idea of blackmailing him or had already been blackmailing him, and had paid the price by being thrown over the side, arms tied, feet bound. The mere detail of proving this and actually exposing the culprits wasn't on Tiff's mind.

In truth, she was probably scared about that side of it, in case she got it wrong or in case somebody prevented her. That was the thing about Tiff. She couldn't handle uncertainty about herself. If she thought that she just might not accomplish something, she didn't try, and yet when she knew she could, she was one of the most devastating people Cat knew.

Cat had steeled herself for the idea that she was going to go to the cabin that night. As such, she was lying in her bed, jeans still on, white jumper around her, looking up at the ceiling. The skies were clear outside and through the cabin window she could see the white landscape, pristine like some showpiece from a winter holiday brochure. That was the real trouble, wasn't it? They were so far away. If she got proof and got it to Scott, then he would be revealed one way or the other. He'd either assist or he would be part of those who were committing the actions. Cat's heart beat fast. She knew which one she hoped it was, because part of her was falling for this man as well. He was so utterly charming and reminded her of Luigi.

Yes, Luigi was reckless, enjoyed a good time, but he'd been devoted to Cat. When his family had said no to him marrying her, he'd done it, anyway. After all, he was the firstborn. He was the king. From his father's death, he was in charge. *Damn the heart defect that took him*, she thought. *I could be living this life with him.*

Maybe that was it. Was she on the rebound? Was it the fact that she had no one now? Had she not addressed that gap? The funeral had been so close and the break off from his family so severe that when her own family didn't want her back, she just went to hell for leather, off to the newest adventure. Well, it was turning out to be quite an adventure, wasn't it?

There came a knock at the door. It wasn't loud or forceful but a gentle tap, as if no one should really hear it. Cat threw back the covers and walked over, opening the door slightly to see who was outside. She recognised the frame and the smile of the man she'd been with earlier that night.

'You said you wanted to go into the cabin. I'll come with you. Again, if anything goes wrong, I can always cover for you. Make up some story about Tiff, who disappeared out of the cabin, and you thought she might be in there. That would work better than your going off on your own getting caught by the captain.'

A hand came out, touching hers. She looked up into a smile that would have melted her as a teenager. It was still having the effect, but there was that slightly older head which had been burned before. The plan was solid. If she did get caught, she now had an excuse. Maybe that was the best thing to do. It would be a risk. Surely it was one worth taking. Cat simply nodded and stepped outside her own cabin.

Quietly, they took the small flight of stairs up towards the owner's cabin. It was at the end of the guest cabins and towards the upper deck of the ship. It was still hidden away, tucked underneath the bridge above. Cat wondered what access it would have up to that bridge. Did the owner have a direct method of getting there? Was she getting too far ahead of herself? Did they build ships like that?

Tiff would know. That was the thing about Tiff. She was like a walking encyclopaedia. She knew such random stuff, but Cat was committed now and onward she went. Once they reached the cabin, Cat went to punch in the pin number but then stopped. *I don't know that, do I?* she thought. *Let's not give away my hand.*

Turning around to her partner, she said, 'So, how do we get in? Captain Jollye punched in a code. Do you know it?' The first officer looked at her, smiled, and gently tapped the code in. He pushed open the door, looking around inside. The cabin was dark with the only light coming from the moonlit side, but it was enough to see by. There was also some light on the exterior of the ship that came in through the large windows. Even though the curtains were drawn, they were not enough to stop this light bathing the room in a very dim, but helpful glow.

'I'll look around,' said Cat. 'See what I can find. Why don't you stand at the door?' Cat walked along the small suite of furniture, looking inside cupboards. This was the bedroom, but she could find no files. Instead, a range of clothing seemed to occupy every drawer. There was the gun still in the wardrobe, but other than that she found no evidence of the mishap that had befallen Ernest Hughes. Every now and again she would turn, and she saw Scott watching her, smiling, gazing at her. He really was quite handsome and was putting it all on the line for her. It had been a while since someone had done that.

Luigi had done that against his family. It was one thing that changed a man from being just a rather good-looking stud to have on your arm, to being a potential mate. Cat could feel a tear in her eye. This was not the time to be thinking about that. Not the time for what she had lost to come back. She needed to focus. She was here for a reason.

Tiff would be better at this. She'd methodically search through everything. No doubt find out the one thing that was important. Having reached the end of the furniture and realising that outside of the gun there was nothing in this room but clothing, Cat strolled back over to the door and leaned up to whisper in the ear of Scott Jones. 'I think I need to go through to the next room. I think that's an office in there.'

'That is indeed his office where he would do his work, but I thought you wanted to check the bag to make sure there was a body in there?'

'You're right,' said Cat quietly. Leaning down, she started to unzip the bag slowly, preparing herself for the face of a dead man. This time she'd check if he was breathing. This time she'd see, but as she did it, she thought she heard something behind her. Turning around, she looked and saw Scott smiling back.

He had her back. There was no need to worry. The guy was obviously sound, and part of her felt this huge relief, but also a little excitement that she could be on the verge of something new with him.

Zipping down the bag, she found herself smiling, a warm glow coming through her. She didn't realise this was totally inappropriate, given the fact she was about to look at a dead man. As she pulled the zip down, she realised something was wrong. She placed her hand inside. As it touched what should have been a body, she heard a crinkle. Her hand shot round the bag, more crinkling and more. It was paper. The entire body bag seemed to be stacked out with paper. She turned to tell Scott, and the man was standing right in front of her. A hand came up, and a cloth was placed across her nose and mouth. Cat's eyes flew wide open and the smile that told of interest and love had changed. There was a devious grin. In the seconds before she blacked out, she swore she heard a quiet, gentle laugh.

Created with Sketch.

Everything was dark. Cat was coming to, but the world wasn't following. She felt clammy sweat across her. When she moved her chin, she felt the roll neck of the jumper. She tried to move her feet, but they were tied together somehow. She wanted to bring her hands across, but they too were tied together in front of her. She could flex her fingers, but her arms wouldn't budge.

There was a rope across her chest. She could feel that much. Her mind started replaying her last moments before she'd ended up here. She heard that little laugh. Saw the grin, the wicked smile. He had baited her, played on her romantic feelings for him. Tiff had been right.

And what about Tiff? Where was she? A sudden urge to find and protect her niece caused her to try to pry apart the bonds that held her, but it was no use. As she desperately looked around, she realised there was a small hole just above her head. The zip had been carelessly done. Pulled right to the top. Cat leaned her head back, trying to wedge her nose into the gap. She wanted to scream, but her mouth was gagged tight. Part of her thought if she did try to scream, giving only a muffled effort, they would come over to silence her, put her out of her misery or at least knock her out again. She would need to be careful.

Cat managed to wedge her nose into the small gap and started to push the zip down as best she could. It was slow work. One set of teeth springing apart at a time. It must have taken her a good five minutes to open up the smallest of gaps. If she lifted her head up, moved one of her eyes across, she could see a small part of the cabin. It was how she had left it. The light was still dim, and she wondered how long she'd been out for. Possibly a while, maybe a few hours, maybe longer. They were quite far north so the light would come early as it had disappeared late in the evening. So where would that put it? *Where would it be on the clock?* she thought. This must be early morning. Early morning before the sun rises. Maybe we're even at five o'clock.

She wondered if they had gone for Tiff in the night. Maybe she was around here, too. Cat tried to roll, but she could see nothing else. The door opened. It was Captain Jollye. She wasn't wearing her smart uniform. Instead, she had a silk dressing gown on. One that ran down to mid-thigh, leaving bare legs underneath. She was still looking at someone across the room. Cat struggled to turn her head to look at the door that went through to Ernest Hughes's study. Jollye was smiling, pushing her hair back; with one hand, she beckoned someone forward.

A man in his mid-thirties, with tightly clipped hair and looking in reasonable shape, stepped across to her. There was a smile across his face and he took the Captain in his arms. Cat watched as they kissed and realised this was no chance encounter. These two had been here before. *It must be Ernest,* thought Cat. *Jollye had said she'd been close to him. Was she doing all this for him? Was this set up by him?* For two minutes they stood there, and then Jollye's dressing gown fell to the ground. The man seemed to want to go further, but Jollye pointed to the other door, picking up her gown, and the pair walked through. Cat heard the door close behind them.

She lay in the darkness hearing noises of lovers from the other room. *Do people really make that much noise?* she thought. And then remembered herself and Luigi. How in a moment like this could you blush? There was no one to watch, and yet she did. The sweat started moving down her face from being inside the bag. She was sticky underneath her jumper, and her jeans were starting to glue to her legs. She needed to get out. Once again, she tilted her head back and tried to push the zip down with her nose. One set of teeth, another set of teeth. *Catriona, keep going. Come on.*

She could hear her mother's voice. It came from her sports days at school. She'd gone to a proper primary school. Oh yes, to educate little ladies, but she remembered those sports days, how she'd always been pretty rubbish. Cat was not of an athletic build, or of an athletic mind. Her mother always said to her, 'You keep going. You don't stop and give up. You are a Munroe.' *Yes,* she thought. *I'm a Munroe with an e. We are not a part of the clan, despite what Dad says. We are just frauds.*

She lay back down, resting her neck. This was no good. She couldn't think like this, she had to keep working. She now had a space with the zip that allowed her to almost get her nose and the top part of her mouth out.

She needed to do more. She needed to work her zip all the way down and try to roll out. Maybe then she could somehow stumble out into the corridor, hop her way down. Something. Get to the guests.

*Come on*, she said to herself. *Nose up. Push.* Her nose caught in the zip. Not once, not twice, but three times. She tried to yelp, but the bind in her mouth stopped any noise from emerging. Next door, they were still heavily occupied, and Cat worked hard, pushing down on the zip until she'd freed enough of it to be able to place her nose, mouth, and chin out. She heard a door opening.

She dropped her head back down and lay there, wondering what was coming. She heard someone ferret about, and then they walked over, the sound of their footsteps on the floor. It wasn't that they were noisy. In fact, the sound was quite indistinct, very gentle, but Cat could feel the presence coming towards her.

Suddenly, there was a hand on the zip, and it was slowly being pulled down the body bag. She saw a pair of fingers move inside, right beside her face, and then another set.

Then the bag was pulled back, as she stared up into the face of the quiet infiltrator in the room.

# Chapter 18

Cat looked up and saw the face of a highly disappointed Tiff. She was shaking her head, looking down at her aunt. 'I did tell you,' she whispered, 'he was no good. You should have stayed away from him. Good job I came to find you.'

Cat went to reply, but then realised that she was still gagged. Her arms couldn't move, and neither could her feet. All she had were her eyes, which were blinking fiercely, hopefully explaining that she needed released.

'I take it that's them I can hear, the captain and Ernest,' whispered Tiff. 'Pretty noisy, aren't they? Sounds quite frisky for a dead man.' Tiff had that grin on her face, the one that said 'I told you so.' The one that said 'I'm cleverer than everyone.' At times she was, although Cat could think of a lot of instances when Tiff wasn't. Unlike Cat, who was more street savvy and comfortable in social situations, Tiff ignored those situations, focusing instead on what she could deal with. Which really said something, when you think she was crawling around a ship in the middle of nowhere. And in the owner's room, albeit an owner who was meant to be dead, but who at this moment, was proving the very opposite to the captain of the ship.

'I guess you want out. Hang on.' Tiff unzipped the bag slowly, not making a sound as she pulled back both sides, Catriona sat up and Tiff reached behind the back of her head untying the knots that held the cloth across her mouth. Once it was free, Cat tried not to spit, tried not to make a sound, but she did shake her hair. Well, it had been tied up too; no doubt it looked creased.

'Can you get my feet and my arms as well? And then the hands?' Tiff nodded and slowly started to work on the knots.

'We need to be in there,' said Tiff, 'that's where the evidence will be, in that room. We need to find out why he's so worried about the blackmail?'

'And then do what?' said Cat. 'This isn't like those mysteries on TV. We're not going to assemble everyone in the stateroom and you can strut around telling everyone their business and how so-and-so wanted so-and-so dead. We need to get the authorities here. How are we going to do that?'

Tiff never batted an eyelid. 'Send a distress signal.'

'A distress signal? What, like with smoke? How are you going to do that?'

'You know nothing about boats. You can send a ship security alert. You send that off, there's other distress messages too that can go up by satellite. I'll need to get to the bridge to do all these things, and then we'll need to disable the communications.'

Cat, now that her arms were free, shrugged her shoulders. Tiff was talking like this was the most common knowledge going. As far as Cat was aware, you got on a boat, somebody drove it. You got some cocktails while onboard, then you got off again. You might go for a swim, but certainly, as for the rest of us, those nice people in the white, with the big caps, they drove the boat.

'I don't understand,' said Cat. 'If you set off all these alarms, well, surely, they'll just call; they've got a radio up there, haven't they? They could just call them, and the captain will go, "No, it's fine—it's all a false alert."'

'Exactly,' said Tiff, 'That's why I need to sabotage everything. We need to send the signal, sabotage it. It's a distress signal, they'll come. They don't not come, and we're not that far away. They could send a helicopter here quite easily.'

'What's the helicopter going to do?' said Cat. 'Even if somebody comes down off it, they can convince those people, can't they? Well, if they do that, what's going to happen then?' Her legs were now free, and she swung round off the bed, standing up, a little wobbly.

'That's your job,' said Tiff. 'You've got to convince everyone that you know what's going on. You need to take charge. I can do all the technical stuff because I'm talented, but you need to talk to people. They may have to mutiny and take over the vessel. Then when they come to get us, we'll be all right.'

'Take over the boat? Cause a mutiny? We don't even know who's who, and who is on what side.'

'We know they're going to be looking for us,' said Tiff. 'We need to see how they keep that quiet. We'll have to sneak about this boat and make sure no one can find us. We'll also have to work out who to trust. Maybe I should do that. You've already got screwed over by the first officer.'

Cat stared at Tiff, her eyes ablaze. Yes, she was right, but this was not the time to bring up things like that. Cat could still read people better than Tiff; she'd just made a mistake. She'd just been lost in a moment of finding someone who might just have been like Luigi. Really, the first thing they had to do was to get out of this cabin because it sounded like the gymnastics next door were coming to an end.

'We need to get out of the room,' said Cat. 'We can't head back to our room either. Have you got everything you need from it?'

Tiff nodded, 'Of course, you won't need much; it's all hairbrushes and stuff. I assume you don't want to do your hair right now.'

Cat wanted to do her hair. Cat wanted to sit down, give it a good brush, then go for a shower. Then come out, dry down, brush it some more, take a couple of hours to sit down in a seat with a nice cocktail in hand and relax. The last couple of hours had not been good. As that was out of the question, she began to think about where to go.

'When should we go to the bridge, Tiff? If you need to be up there, what's the best way to do that?'

'Sooner, rather than later,' said Tiff. 'When it becomes daylight, there will be more people walking about. It's already five, but once we do it,' said Tiff, 'I don't know where we go. I don't know where we hide out.'

Catriona ushered her sister towards the door. 'I have an idea,' she said. 'There's one person who I think has played straight the whole time. We'll go there.' Tiff opened the cabin door gently and peered out into the hall. But then she threw her head back inside.

'There's somebody out there,' Tiff said. 'Someone in the corridor.'

'Who?'

'I'm not sure.'

'Well, is it a man? Is it a woman? What are they wearing?' added Cat.

'It seems to be a coat, but with bare legs.'

'What colour's the hair?' said Catriona. *It was difficult, infuriating, when Tiff didn't answer fully.* There was also movement in the cabin next door, and they could be discovered at any time.

'She's got blonde hair.'

'About my size?' Tiff nodded. 'Right,' says Catriona. 'That's Fragrance. I think she's spying on them. She knows something's up as well. Have a quick look, see if she's going because they're making more noise next door. Sounds like they're about to come in here or out there.'

Tiff opened the door and after looking left and right along the corridor, she stuck her head back in. 'She's gone.'

'Go,' said Cat. 'Go.' Stepping outside, they closed the door, and then Tiff looked at Cat.

'Where do we go?' she said.

'The bridge. You said you needed to go to the bridge. Yes?'

'Yes,' said Tiff. 'That'll be up this way. I can head up into it if you want.'

'Well, I'm coming with you. I can hardly hang about. Get up, do what you have to do, and then we're going.'

Tiff made her way along the corridor straight past Ernest Hughes's workroom. Cat prayed that nobody would come out, but also prayed they wouldn't go into the other room. Maybe having had such a good time, they might just relax, stay in his workroom. But Cat was unsure, so she stuck close to Tiff, urging her on.

They had to go up some round steps to get up to the level of the bridge. Once up at the highest point of the boat, they looked into the dimly lit control room. Slowly, Tiff crept forward, Cat holding on behind her. Cat thought she could see a radar screen, another screen that she thought was possibly clouds and weather. There was a radio of some sort and another radio over on the far wall. It wasn't the biggest bridge she'd ever seen. The last time she'd been on a bridge, it had been a tour of a warship. It certainly looked different to this. This was snappier, cleaner in some ways, more elegant, but then again, she guessed, it had to be less practical.

'What you want me to do, Tiff?'

Tiff turned and glared at her aunt. 'Just make sure no one's coming. I don't think you would know how to destroy any of this I want to do. I'm just going to look for the button, send the alert from that. I'll send off the distress alerts, as well, and then I'm going to start cutting everything, pulling it apart. I have to make a good job of it.'

Cat nodded and looked around for the exits from the bridge. One went on to a rear upper deck, small with a drop ladder down onto the deck below. The other exit being through the circular staircase they'd come up. It was hard to see both areas from the same position, so Cat decided she would move slowly from one to the other, keeping her ears open.

Occasionally, she would look at Tiff, who seemed to have pressed one of the buttons, and was knowingly standing over a radio. It was twenty minutes, twenty minutes of walking back and forward, listening intently, but there was no one on the bridge. Cat was sure that there was a watch on the bridge most times. Certainly, on the warship, they'd said that, that the bridge was manned 24/7. Then she guessed, with something like this, you were right in the middle of nowhere. They hadn't seen another boat since she'd been on the vessel. Maybe that counted for something. Maybe you didn't need to have a watch then for the whole time, or maybe Captain Jollye was meant to be on watch while she was partaking in her extracurricular activities with a dead man.

Cat nearly jumped when Tiff tapped the back of her shoulder. 'What?'

'I'm done,' said Tiff. 'I've cut all the connections, I've ripped them apart underneath, sent off all the distress signals before that, so they should be coming. I just want to find the EPIRB and throw it in.'

'The what?' said Cat.

'The EPIRB. The Emergency Positioning Indicating Radio Beacon; it's for when the boat goes down. If it hits the water, it sends a satellite signal, a distress signal, so they'll come looking for it. There'd be no doubt that we're in trouble because I'm sending everything. I've also killed all the internet. At the moment, we're dead in the water. We cannot receive or send anything—Wi-Fi, the lot.'

'Well, that'll be interesting. We'll see how the captain explains that one away. If she does, of course,' said Cat. Something in her mind was trying to send a message. *Had they overplayed this? Would the captain wait for the emergency vessels to arrive? Surely, she wouldn't sink her own boat and just take everybody out that was on it. No, that would be too much. How would they escape? Where they were was causing a problem for everyone.*

'How far are we from help?' asked Cat.

'I would say it would take a good couple of hours to get here, at least,' said Tiff, 'Get themselves into gear, realise this is a distress, try to contact us. They could be coming anything from about four hours onwards.'

'Then we have four hours to clear this up, four hours to have evidence when people arrive, but we need to plan what we're going to do next. So, we're going for your EPIRB, and then we go and hide until we see what happens when they know we're missing.'

Tiff led Cat out of the rear door of the bridge, down the steps, onto the open deck. While Cat stayed in the corner, Tiff walked nonchalantly around looking for the EPIRB. It was as if nothing was afoot. Her mind solely focused on one task. There was a beauty in her, that she could be so single-focused, be it from a condition or the way she was, but there was also a frailness in that she ignored the rest of the outside world at her peril. If someone caught her now, they wouldn't be lenient.

At that point, Tiff turned around and stuck her thumb up in the air. Cat saw her pick up what seemed to be quite a large device and simply toss it off the side. With that, she ran back over to Cat. 'So where are we going? Where do we hide out? It's such a small boat.'

'We need to go down,' said Cat, 'See if anyone's in the stateroom, if not, through there, into the galley.'

'The galley?' said Tiff, 'How are we going to hide in the kitchen?'

'The only people that ever go into the galley are the chef, and those who serve at serving time, and the one person on this boat who's warned me about anything has been that chef. If there's anyone we're going to trust, it's going to be Mr Popov.' Tiff looked at Cat. At first, her eyes were bright and raised, then she seemed to cock her head as if she were thinking about it.

'I haven't met him,' said Tiff, 'So I reckon we'll have to go with it. I wouldn't trust anyone else.' And with that, Tiff started to walk off to find the steps down to the stateroom.

'Where are you going? You could be seen quite easily going down there.'

'There's one route down, and yes, it's open, but it's half-five six in the morning, and this is the best chance to get down there without being seen. You wait any longer, and people start going for breakfast. You need to relax. We've got this,' said Tiff. With that, she marched off. Cat walked quickly after her, but her gait was not so nonchalant. *Need to relax. There's a murderer on board. Someone is dead. We're going to be hunted. I was stuck in a black body bag. And, by the way, dear niece,* Cat said in her mind, *I'm also still as sticky as anything from being stuck in that bag. Flipping heck, I stink.*

The route to the stateroom was clear. Tiff picked up a couple of items of fruit as they made their way over to the galley. Walking down the galley steps, Cat looked around the stainless-steel kitchen to see anywhere to hide.

'Over here,' she said to Tiff and pulled open a large cupboard at about knee-height. 'I think that we can squeeze in here if we shove these pots this way and those that way.' There wasn't a lot of room as the pair crawled inside, and once they'd shut the door, Tiff and Cat found their knees sitting right up against their faces.

'And we just wait here?' said Tiff, 'How are we going to solve the rest of the case? We're going to have to move about.'

'But you're going to need people out of their cabins for that,' said Cat. 'When the life of this ship starts to move again, then we'll be able to do something. We need to see the lay of the land over the next hour.'

Then there came the sound of footsteps. A whistling accompanied them, a tune Cat did not recognise, but it sounded military. Lots of good up and down beats in a standard time. The tune stopped right in front of the cupboard the girls were hiding in. She heard the crack of a knee as someone bent down, and then the cupboard was opened.

'Ah, I warned you to be careful, but here you are. You hide in my cupboard.'

# Chapter 19

Catriona breathed a sigh of relief as she saw the Russian chef before her. He was crouched down, looking inside the cupboard at the two women squashed up together, and gently moved a pan handle from Catriona's face.

'I think it best you don't come out. I thought I heard someone about,' said Mr Popov. 'Give me a moment to make sure and I'll be back.' With that, he shut the cupboard door, leaving the girls in darkness again.

'Can we trust him?' said Tiff quietly. 'I mean, can you really trust him?'

'He was the one who warned us, or he warned me; probably be lucky to get a word in with you.'

'What's that meant to mean?'

'What it's meant to mean,' said Catriona, 'is you need to switch on all the time, make some friends; you can't simply just charge around in your own world.'

'I don't. I do things when it's necessary. I just have never seen it as being very necessary to talk to a Russian chef. Neither did I see it necessary to flirt with the first officer who's obviously up to his neck in this.'

'Don't. Just don't!' said Catriona, and she went no further for fear that she would start a row that could be heard throughout the ship. That was the thing with Tiff. You start off trying to accuse her of something and she would round on it, instantly, brazenly, as if she were deeply offended for ever being accused of anything in the first place. But there was no time for that. Their lives really were in danger, felt Catriona. If they were caught at the moment, who knows what would happen to them?

Clearly not everybody on the ship was in on this. What was it exactly? It seemed that blackmail had been on the cards. Was that why Earnest Hughes had called all these people onto the boat? Was he trying to find out who was blackmailing him? Certainly, it seemed that Jack Fogherty had reason to approach him; whether that turned into blackmail was unclear. Mrs Bridge was obviously suspected of doing something irregular, having had her goods searched. The professor—he also knew Mr Hughes well. Sarah Gosling, surely she was innocent here. A millionaire, a lucky lottery winner now bringing the man of her dreams along and probably finding out he wasn't much of a dreamboat after all. As for the crew, Mr Popov seemed, if not trustworthy, at least not in cahoots with the rest of the crew. As for the others, the captain clearly was and so was the first officer but the other two, well Tara Limpet had been with Jack Fogherty before he died. Was she involved? And who knew about Mr Denny? As for Demi Forsyth, she was a prime suspect to be involved in this, a dead man's PA, or not-so-dead man. Just where did Catriona go next?

There were footsteps now in the kitchen again and Catriona braced herself, ready to lash out a foot if an unfriendly face appeared at the cupboard entrance. The steps came closer, and they sounded heavy, thickset. Surely this was Popov. The cupboard doors opened directly and there was the Russian's bald but smiling face. You could smell the drink off of him, and Catriona wondered just how he kept his job. His hand reached in, and she took it, climbing out of the cupboard, followed by Tiff. She shrugged her shoulders, working her neck, before reaching up and running her fingers through her hair. It was a mess, but it was going to have to do. Maybe she should tie it up. She looked across at Tiff. Tiff had long brown hair. Very straight, no curls. How was it that Tiff's hair looked immaculate? She didn't even try. That was the annoying thing.

'I take it you're okay,' said Mr Popov. 'I don't think anyone will be about for a bit, but I need to start making the lunch soon, and when that happens, Mr Denny will be here coming back and forward, assisting me. You don't want to be here when that happens. You will need to go.'

Catriona nodded. The man's English was good, but it was slow, stuttered, as if he had to think about it. But then she thought about her Russian. She couldn't even think about that, never mind stutter her way through it.

'Mr Popov, thank you. I didn't know where else to go. You seem to be someone on the lookout, someone worried about me, about us—thank you.'

The man nodded. 'Your daughter,' he said 'I seen her type before. She get herself into trouble, but she means well, and she very clever.'

'She's not my daughter. My niece, my brother's daughter.' The man's face showed incomprehension, but he smiled anyway.

'A good-looking woman like you. I don't want to see nice looking woman in trouble.'

'Well, thank you,' said Catriona, 'but I'm not sure what we do next. We came here to hide and you tell me we can't. Why do you think there's such trouble? What do you know, Mr Popov?' The man turned around, walked across the small galley, and grabbed a bottle from the side. The liquid in it was clear. Catriona guessed it was vodka.

'You want one?' Catriona thought that maybe she should keep a clear head, but inside her stomach was churning. They were really up against it here. This was for real. Someone was dead. She nodded.

'And your little niece?'

'She never takes. It's fine,' said Catriona. 'Just me.'

'Good. Let me make it a decent one.' Two glasses went down on the table. Tumblers, not shot glasses. Catriona watched as the liquid was filled half the way up.

'It'll stiffen you up, get you ready to do what you have to do.' And with that, the man took his tumbler before handing one to Catriona. She looked up, watched the man down the contents of the glass in one go before giving his head a little shake. 'It's not the best vodka,' he said, 'but it will do. It all does. Drink up.'

Catriona looked down at the clear liquid. People should not be mistaken. Catriona liked her drink. She especially liked her cocktails, and she could drink with the best of them. This was neat, and this was half a tumbler. Oh, what the heck? She needed to keep in this guy's good books. The tumbler went to her lips. She threw her head back and downed the vodka. There was a raging fire running up her throat, and she fought hard not to cough. Handing the tumbler back to Popov, she gave a faint smile.

'Ah. You're the sort of woman I like. Determined. Won't be shown up, and you can drink. If I were twenty years younger, you and I would make a great team.'

Catriona wasn't so sure about that, but she knew how to keep a man engaged, and flicked her hair back. At least the man wasn't lecherous. He was fun, direct, but he was also helpful.

At the moment, that was what she needed. 'How long have you been on this ship?' asked Catriona.

'I new crew,' said Popov. 'The previous chef, he went sick, so they were pretty desperate, but I could make good food. I was a chef in a restaurant in Moscow. Top chef before they sacked me.'

'What did they sack you for?' asked Catriona.

'Because he drank too much. Didn't make it on time. Food came out late.' Catriona shot a look at Tiff. She might be right, she might be wrong, but this man was helping them.

'Ha ha. You look at her with such annoyance, but she is right. I couldn't handle my drink. I turned up late. They sacked me, but only after fifth time. Because my food's so good, they did not want me to be sacked.'

'You don't really know any of the crew?'

'No,' said Popov, 'but I watch them. I watch them a lot. The captain and Mr Hughes, very close. As in bunkie-bunkie close. Yes, you understand? The first officer, he close with money. The other two, I don't think they are close at all.'

'I'm not so sure,' said Catriona. 'I saw Tara with Jack Fogherty not long before he died.'

'Oh, yes,' said Popov. 'Tara, Tara, she like—how do you say it? Game girl, but a lovely, lovely girl. Not a bad bone in her body. I know this. She very helpful for me, but she not in anybody's pay. Her and Denny both still quite new. The others not so.'

'But she faked the gun accident. They were all over there. None of the guests were around when the gun accident happened. The one they said killed Mr Hughes.'

'Mr Hughes is not dead,' said Popov. 'He upstairs. Him and the captain make too much noise. Mr Denny, Tara, too young, too naïve. But I think it, about first officer, captain, I know something going on. I know something happening because the gun was not a fake. The gun accident was real. But also, I overhear people. You see, I'm Russian. My speech, not good, therefore, people think I know nothing. Thick, but I am not thick.'

Catriona put her hand out onto the man's hairy hand and gave him a smile. 'No, you're not thick. You warned me. You've now saved my life.'

'I don't think I saved your life. I think I warned you. You still got ahead. Now you're in my cupboard. I warn you, so you stay out and you get back to land safe. Now you're in big trouble.' Catriona blushed somewhat as she realised the man was probably right, but that wasn't her, and it certainly wasn't Tiff.

'And your niece, she very clever. She watches, but then she says things in public before people. Not good. You need to control her.'

'I don't need controlled,' said Tiff. 'I know what I'm doing. I'm going to solve this.'

'You see? I understand. She don't see the world completely, does she? She don't understand the world. She reveals stuff to these people, they kill her.'

Catriona stopped in her tracks somewhat. 'Yes, they'll kill her. They'll kill me, too. They would kill you as well if they find us here, yes?'

'Yes. Also understand something happening. Not all Mr Hughes. Mr Hughes doing thing for reason. Mr Hughes not nice man. He has strange liaisons. He has contracts, businesses, that are not so good, so he have enemies. Enemies onboard, enemies are dangerous. I don't want to see you or even your niece get hurt. You understand?'

'Yes,' said Cat, running her hands through her hair. 'I understand, but it may be too late.' She saw the Russian furrow his brow with questioning eyes. 'We have called the authorities,' said Catriona. 'We set off the ship alarms, and Tiff knows how to do it. I think we need people here and you and I will all be safe.'

The Russian looked slightly horrified, but then he shook his shoulders. Taking a tumbler, he put it down, looked at Catriona and set her tumbler down. Quickly, he poured himself half a tumbler, and then started to pour one for Catriona, but he stopped about a quarter of the way up. Taking the tumblers, he handed one to Catriona. 'This time I not give you half. You need clear head, therefore, only quarter. Here, to you solving what happens and being alive at the end and if you're alive, I cook your special meal. You dress up nice, I cook meal. Nothing else. I just like to make food for a nice lady.' With that, the Russian dropped the tumbler full of vodka.

*Well, somebody's good to me*, thought Catriona, and her vodka followed suit. Taking the tumblers, Popov placed them on the side and put the top back on the vodka. As he went to wash the tumblers, he suddenly stopped, his ear half-cocked to the ceiling above him.

'Someone's on the way,' he said. 'Quick, we need to hide you.' Catriona went to get back in the cupboard, but she felt a Russian arm pulling her away. 'No,' he said 'Not there. I take you over here. A freezer. It's safer. When they gone, I open it. You go elsewhere. But they'll be here very soon.'

The man strode across the small galley and pulled open a metal door. Cat saw the cold air inside coming out like a mist. Grabbing Tiff, she dragged her inside the small freezer. They were able to stand upright but were so close that their noses were almost touching. As the door closed, everything went dark. Outside the freezer, they could hear a voice, 'Popov, are you still drinking? If we were back on land, you'd be off this boat. That's enough. The captain says she wants lunch brought forward, so get on to it. Have you seen the Contessa with her girl?'

'A girl?' whispered Tiff indignantly. Cat's hand flew up to Tiff's mouth covering it and she pulled her niece close. Cat was starting to shiver in the cold.

'I just have a warmer. I am fine. I make food, no problem. Tell captain not to worry. She will have her food.'

'Have you seen the Contessa? I was looking for her.'

'Oh, yes? I hear the rest of crew say you after her.'

'Well,' said the voice, now clearly identifiable as First Officer Jones, 'she's a bit of stuff, nice bit of rough to handle.'

Inside, Catriona was indignant. If she saw him next time, she'd plant her knee between his legs, sort the man out.

'So, have you seen them?' asked Scott Jones.

'No, I've been in galley. I've been in galley I have my drink. I'm making food I serve breakfast. This is what I do on the boat. I see no one. No one come through here. Next person I see, Mr Denny. The guests don't come in galley. You know that. That's why I stay here.'

'Well, okay, but upstairs, Captain wants her lunch, but she wants to see you first, just a quick word.'

'Okay. I go captain.' With that, Catriona could hear the Russian walking out of the galley.

Tiff went to speak, but Catriona kept her hand over her mouth tight. She hadn't heard Scott Jones leave, and she certainly wasn't going to take a chance. She was then proved right, as she heard a vodka bottle being unscrewed and a tumbler being filled. Cheeky blighter was taking the Russian's drink.

'Where are you, you wee bitch?' said Scott Jones, muttering under his breath. 'You and that other one? All you had to do was play it right. A bit of rumpy-pumpy. Everyone's shut up and back on the land after. Women, especially these sorts of aristocratic women, just can't behave themselves. Nice filly, but not one you want in the stable.'

Catriona felt like she was about to explode. Filly, he called her a filly, more than that, one not for his stable. Well, she wouldn't go in his stable, anyway, and she was one horse he certainly couldn't tame. He continued with this ridiculous sexist metaphor, and then Cat felt Tiff holding her tight. Tiff was obviously aware of what the man had said. Pulling her aunt close. Tiff knew that Catriona had felt something for this man, really felt something. Maybe there was some emotional maturity in there. Maybe she did really care. Tiff held tight until they heard the footsteps of Scott Jones leaving the galley.

'Thank you, Tiff. I needed that.'

'What? I was cold. You're warm, I was cold, but now we need to get out of here.'

It dawned on Catriona that Tiff had not had any emotional maturity. She was just feeling cold. Really? She missed all that?

'How do we get out of here?'

'Well, there's a dead man's lock, surely,' said Tiff. 'Probably set off an alarm or something.'

'No,' said Catriona. 'The alarm goes, we're dead.'

'Then it looks like we're trapped,' said Tiff. 'I might have to get us out of here because I'm cold.'

# Chapter 20

Catriona shivered. She was unsure just how long she could stay in the freezer; surely Popov would be back soon. He'd only been sent upstairs to see the captain, unless of course, they knew something. Maybe he wouldn't be back; maybe Jollye would dispose of him.

The image of Jack Fogherty's body kept coming to Catriona. At times she struggled to believe that anyone on board was actually a killer, but clearly, someone was. Popov seemed to believe that there was a murderer on the other side. Of course, he could have been playing them. Maybe that's why they're in the freezer. Maybe he's not intending to come back; that would be a handy way to get rid of the pair of them.

Girls running around, ending up in the freezer, froze themselves to death. No, she couldn't believe that of the Russian. He was too nice; he had complimented her. He seemed to have that almost fatherly fondness for her, an old man with daft dreams. Or was that all an act?

'Cat, what are we going to do?'

'We wait for Popov,' said Catriona. 'We wait for Mr Popov to come back and open the door. If we set the alarm off, we don't know who's going to open it.'

'But it's cold,' said Tiff. 'I don't like the cold. I'm getting cold all up my legs, up to my top, everything; I mean everything.'

'Everything's cold to me as well,' said Catriona. 'You just have to grin and bear it. He'll be back; the man's looked after us. Now shush.' With that, Catriona embraced Tiff, but Tiff didn't make any effort at all to embrace back. Maybe Catriona was no longer warm—certainly, her face didn't feel it. She was sure there was a drip on her nose.

'Do you have your phone on you?' said Catriona.

'Of course,' said Tiff.

'Put the light on. We'll see what we can see.' Taking her phone out of her pocket, Tiff flicked on a switch via the smart screen and there was a light suddenly within the room. A large piece of beef looked directly at Catriona. There was some pork on the side. There were boxes which purported to be fish above them. Everywhere, food tightly packed in and this ridiculously small space at the front where a person could stand.

'There's a dead man's alarm there,' said Tiff. 'We could just pull that, then we'll be fine.'

'No,' said Catriona. 'No, no, no. We wait. Just because you're cold. It's better to be cold than dead.'

'I'm going to be frozen to death soon,' said Tiff. 'I mean, why hide us in here? We were fine in the cupboard.'

'We weren't really, we had nowhere to run, nowhere to hide. Who's going to hide somebody in a freezer?'

'That's my point exactly,' said Tiff. 'It's ridiculous.' Cat was unsure of how long they'd been in there, but she decided she wasn't going to stand the whole time and carefully lowered herself down to the floor.

'Tiff, come down here with me.'

'Why?' said Tiff.

'Because I asked you to. For once, can you do what your aunt asks?'

'Now you sound like you're forty-something. You're not that much older than me, you know that.'

'I know that. I'm very aware of that, but I'm also the older one here. Now come down.' Catriona could see the girl starting to shiver badly. As Tiff lowered herself down so that she sat on Catriona's lap, Contessa wrapped her arms around her niece. 'We're going to be all right,' said Catriona. 'It's going to get cold for a bit, but we're going to be fine. Okay?' With that, she nestled her head into Tiff's neck. *The girl must really be feeling the cold*, she thought, *because she's not fighting against the show of affection. She doesn't like to be close to someone. She doesn't like to be held. She must really be struggling.*

Catriona waited for a sign of someone entering the galley. *How long could the captain want Mr Popov? She said she wanted lunch brought forward, so he had to go and make it, but she seemed to be keeping him for a long time. Where would they go when they got out? Because when Mr Popov comes back, she knew they couldn't stay in the galley. They'd have to go elsewhere. Would be best to hide out in somebody's cabin, but who could she trust?*

Heinrich and Fragrance were up to their eyes in this, surely. Jack Fogherty's room could be searched at any time, and it would be locked, so they'd have to get in, in the first place. Harriet Bridge was an option, but as her stuff had been rifled through, maybe she was the blackmailer or the one Hughes was after. Maybe she was just playing it well. They certainly couldn't trust any of the crew, but Sarah Gosling and Tyrrell Kopeck sounded like a good bet. Certainly, Sarah Gosling. After all, she was just here by chance. A lottery winner, who had then brought Mr Kopeck with her, or maybe he suggested it. Maybe it was him. Yes, Sarah seemed the obvious choice.

Catriona held her niece tight, waiting for the footsteps of Mr Kopeck. Her arms began to lose some sensation. She wasn't quite at the stage of having been frozen so that she couldn't move, but things were starting to get extremely uncomfortable.

'Tiff, I think we're going to have to pull that switch. We're going to have to do it. I think if we keep this up, we could end up freezing to death in here. How long has it been?' Tiff didn't respond. 'Are you okay, Tiff?' Catriona slapped the side of Tiff's face, and found her hand knocked away. Yes, she was okay. Just in one of her sulks.

'Stand up, and I'll stand up too, and we'll pull this switch. There's a joint of pork up there we can arm ourselves with and a few other things in case we don't get a friendly face on the other side.' Together, the women stood ready. The light from Tiff's mobile phone highlighting the door in front of them and where the dead man's switch was. Cat stood with a side of beef in one hand, while Tiff held a pork joint. They weren't the best of weapons, but maybe if they threw them and hit the person, they could then run for it.

'Pull the switch, Tiff.' Catriona watched her niece reach forward and yank on the chain. An alarm went off outside the freezer, and Cat heard footsteps almost immediately. She braced herself; tomorrow's Sunday lunch in her hand.

What caught her by surprise was the sudden burst of light as the door opened. She couldn't see who it was, but hurled her beef straight towards the person. She heard it fall to the floor, and a voice moaned.

'What are you doing? They will be coming. Go. Go. I came back for you, but you wouldn't wait. Now go.' Catriona stared in stunned silence at the Russian chef before her, but Tiff was quicker, grabbed Catriona's hand, and ran out up into the stateroom. Casting a last glance over her shoulder, Catriona saw the Russian close the freezer door on himself, locking himself in. The alarm stopped momentarily before starting again. He really was quite clever. She hoped he would be okay.

Emerging through the small steps up into the stateroom, Catriona saw it was empty. Some breakfast food was still on the side as well as some breakfast dishes, but no one was here. The hour must have been round about nine o'clock. Tiff thought themselves fortunate.

'Where do we go?' said Tiff. 'Where do we go?'

'Sarah Gosling's. We need to go to Sarah Gosling's.'

'But if we go up into the guest quarters, we'll be seen,' said Tiff. 'It's pretty obvious that's where we'll go.'

'Up out towards the deck. If we can hide there, we might be able to run in when we know it's clear.' Tiff didn't wait to work out if it was a good idea, instead making off to the open deck at the back. Once they came out into the daylight, Cat could hear the deck above them was occupied. It sounded like Captain Jollye, but she wasn't in a good mood.

'Well, where are they?' she said loudly. 'They've got to be about somewhere. Ernest doesn't pay you to sit around on your arse all day. Get yourself out and about with the crew. Find me those women and do it subtly. I realise there's nothing subtle about you.'

'He'll always prefer the younger woman, you do realise that?' said the voice. Cat clocked it was Demi Forsythe and heard a slap to the face.

'You speak to me like that again, and there will be no younger woman for him to sleep with. Now go.' Cat wasn't of an age when the idea of being the older woman really struck her, but it certainly seemed to annoy the captain. Clearly, she was in love with Mr Hughes. She wanted him all to herself, but he wasn't ready to do that. She was risking a lot, and Cat wondered if she'd kill for him. Somebody killed Jack Fogherty.

'Can you hear those feet?' said Tiff quietly. 'They're coming up from the stateroom.' Cat grabbed her niece and hid behind a fixed bench out on the deck. It would be hard to see them if he came straight out from the stateroom, but if he wandered over, then it would be as clear as day.

'They must be out here somewhere. Contessa?' came the voice. It was Scott Jones, 'Contessa, we need to talk to you. Are you okay? Contessa?' the shout came out. Catriona realised the man was on the deck. She dared not pop her head up above the bench she was hiding behind, otherwise he would see. Tucked down tight behind it, Catriona caught a look of Tiff's face and for once saw fear. She tried to smile reassuringly, but inside her stomach was churning. She believed that if the man came over, she would attack him. She'd go hell for leather to defend her pride, but also to defend her niece, but Catriona was no idiot, she wasn't strong enough to fight her way out of this. Then she had an idea.

The guest quarters ran either side of the ship. If she could climb up to the next deck, but remain on the outside of the ship, she wouldn't be seen, and if she could scuttle along to the window of Sarah Gosling's, she might be able to get in. The windows were generally closed, and certainly she hadn't opened the one in her cabin. But they could open. There were fastenings there to let you open the window fully.

Catriona looked around Tiff to the far end of the deck where she now saw Scott Jones looking out to sea. He then peered over the edge and started looking around it. Maybe he was looking to the deck below right where they put the small rib up to the ship. How long would he be there? This was the time to move. Cautiously, Catriona flipped her head above the bench and saw the rest of the deck was empty. Grabbing Tiff's hand, she quickly ran to the edge of the railings and hoisted herself over before lowering herself down.

There was a general smoothness on the outside of the ship, but there weren't a number of handholds and rails that ran along it. Cat fixed her hands tight to one of these railings and started moving sideways along. As soon as she was clear of the open part of the deck, she decided she needed to move up to the deck above.

Climbing had been a passion of Luigi's and several times, they'd gone out so that Cat understood the basics. She was fortunate enough that she was in reasonable shape and had arms that could at least support her own weight, if not much heavier. What she was wary of was anyone looking over the side of the ship at this time, so they needed to move quickly.

Tiff was a trooper. She hadn't said anything, but simply followed her aunt onto the side of the ship and now, as they scrambled up, she took every handhold her aunt showed her. Catriona was now level with the cabins of the guests. As she moved along, she realised that the first one she'd come to would be that of Harriet Bridge. While not the worst person to be discovered by, she didn't want to be. She peered into the window. Mrs Bridge was inside, at a small desk reading paperwork. Cat turned and gave a wave to Tiff to say that it was time to move. Quickly, she scuttled past the first and the second window of the cabin. Harriet Bridge remained at her desk, facing forward.

'Thank God for that,' said Tiff, as they came upon the cabin of Sarah Gosling. Carefully, she looked into the first window and saw Tyrrell Kopeck. He was giving a back rub to Sarah Gosling, and he didn't seem to be the happiest doing it. She was lying on the bed, her dressing gown pulled back to reveal bare shoulders. The man was massaging her. Cat rapped on the window lightly.

Mrs Gosling rolled off the bed, quickly standing up, desperately wrapping her dressing gown around her. Tyrrell Kopeck stared at the window and then smiled. Cat gave a wave and then pointed to the locks on the window. Tyrrell looked at Sarah Gosling. He seemed to be quite annoyed, but he then came over and started undoing the locks. Maybe Cat had saved him from a fate worse than death. One thing about the man was, he clearly was not enamoured with Mrs Gosling.

The window was opened out, and Tyrrell's face appeared. 'What are you up to out there?' he said. 'I know it's rather bracing, but that's a little off-piste, is it not?'

'We need to come in, Mr Kopeck. Please let me in.'

'By all means. It's not often I get two young women appearing at my window,' and with that, he stepped back, allowing Catriona to wriggle her way into the room.

As she stood up and began to sort herself out, Cat saw Sarah Gosling making for the door. 'I'll just tell the captain you're here. They've been looking all over for you.'

Cat ran across the room and put her hand on the door before Sarah got there, turning the lock. 'No,' she said. 'You need to sit down, and we need to talk. There's something I have to tell you and it's quite shocking.'

# Chapter 21

'Well,' said Mr Kopeck. 'I'm all for a bit of excitement and adventure, especially with you two girls climbing in through the window. Shock me, please do.'

Sarah Gosling looked at Tyrrell Kopeck almost with a slight air of disgust, but Cat noticed a slight tension in her as well. 'What's happening?' said Sarah. 'I don't get this. I'm here on a cruise. You find somebody dead, now you're climbing through windows, what are you doing?'

'I'm sorry,' said Cat, 'and it must be quite shocking for you, but we needed to do this; they're after us at the moment. If anyone comes to that door, don't let on we're here, hide us somewhere. Promise me that, please.' There was an earnestness in Catriona's voice, one that was coming from within, not put on. 'You see, Mr Hughes, he's not dead. I've seen Ernest Hughes alive. There's been some sort of ruse going on and I know you haven't got anything to do with it, Sarah. You've just won your millions and come here, but I think Mr Kopeck's here for a reason, as are the professor, Jack Fogherty and Harriet Bridge. You see, Mr Hughes was being blackmailed by somebody, or at least he thought there was the potential. We reckon it is blackmail, but we haven't got the evidence.'

'What on earth are you talking about?' asked Sarah. 'No evidence, it's just made-up stories, and Mr Hughes, he's dead, he's in his room.'

'No, he's not,' said Tiff. 'Well, maybe he is in his room, but he's up and walking about.'

'Up and walking about? What on earth?' said Sarah.

'Really?' said Tyrrell. 'Mr Hughes is alive. How? I thought they carried him in off that ice?'

'Yes, but who was with him?' said Tiff. 'They've been in on it all along.'

'Easy,' said Catriona. 'Easy. Our two friends here haven't heard the story; we need to take it slower, Tiff. You see, I was grabbed the other night. The first officer, he put me in the room in the body bag that Mr Hughes was meant to be in, but he wasn't and then I saw him with the captain.'

'You saw him with the captain?' said Tyrrell. 'Doing what?'

'Well, I saw them going into a room,' said Catriona. 'I heard what they did after that.'

'This is all a bit saucy, isn't it?' said Tyrrell.

'I'm sure it'll be a lot of fun,' said Cat, 'except that Jack Fogherty is dead. We know that Harriet Bridge had something on Mr Hughes; we know the professor does, too. We also know from being in his room, that Jack Fogherty did and for that reason, we think they were brought here, so Mr Hughes could find out—that's why he faked his death. We reckon that somebody thought that Jack Fogherty was the one doing it; that's why he's gone. A little accident at sea, not difficult.'

'All seems a bit preposterous to me,' said Sarah Gosling, 'I mean, two accidents at sea—how are you going to get away with that?'

'On the contrary, quite easy; to make Mr Hughes seem dead, the blackmailer suddenly has nothing and Mr Hughes gets a lot of time to investigate everyone. People will speak freely, he will be able to find out exactly what they knew. He could search rooms; you know the captain can get into any of these rooms, don't you? He certainly tried getting into ours.' Catriona could see the shock on Tyrrell's face.

'Was there something you wanted to say?' asked Cat. 'Mr Kopeck, is there something you want to say?'

'Well, it's just that, I mean, all his dealings with the production company and stuff, they weren't one hundred percent. Some of these TV movies I've been in, and some contracts we got, we haven't done it completely above board.'

'What do you mean?' asked Tiff, sitting down on the bed. 'You need to explain that one to me.'

'What I mean is, Mr Hughes's mother was a big fan of mine, especially in the younger days, and she kept asking him to put me in in the movies, but things haven't been that good. Since the early successes, it's harder and harder to get work, but he said to me to come with him and he would get me into some "good deals", as he put it. In the end, they turned out to be trashy TV movies, but they all had somebody else lined up for them. Until we had that evening with the producer. I'm not happy about it, and some things done with the girls involved, not by me, but by Mr Hughes and his producer buddy, they're not right. But I was involved, I was there, so I didn't say anything. I got my movies, and I ended up, at least, with some sort of money coming in. But when you said he was looking for someone bent on vengeance, bent on blackmail, I had the ability. I'm not doing it. I wouldn't dream of it. He's too dangerous a man, but I could have if I'd been daft enough.'

'But at the end of the day,' said Cat, 'you were here by chance. I mean, Mrs Gosling's the one who paid to come on the boat. She was the one who brought you here.'

'Still awfully suspicious,' said Tiff. 'That doesn't sound right to me.'

'Well, this is all just confusing,' said Sarah. 'I didn't want this. I won my millions. All I wanted to do was to come away with the man of my TV dreams, who turns out to be after every other bit of skirt in the place except me. Now we've got dead bodies and people climbing in through my room. Well, I'm not happy about it. I'm not. I think we'll need to go to the captain.'

'You can't,' said Tiff. 'The captain is at the centre of this. Do you understand why we came to you? Because you're not involved. We need people who are not involved.'

'Easy, Tiff,' said Cat. 'But she's right, we need people who are not involved. We need to be able to subdue what's going on. There may be members of the crew not involved. We don't know.'

Cat saw Tiff about to say something but held her hand up in front of her. The last thing she wanted was Popov's name being put out there. Always best to play your cards close to your chest. She knew he was an ally. She didn't want to give him up, realising that some people she was talking to may not be. 'But the first officer is definitely in on it. That slime ball,' said Cat.

'He was certainly all over you,' said Kopeck. 'I could see that. Don't blame him, mind.'

Sarah Gosling hit Tyrrell in the arm. 'You're here for me. You do realise that, don't you? You don't need to insult me in front of everyone else.'

'We need to stop this,' said Cat. 'At the moment, we need

to go and expose Mr Hughes. Bring him out into the open so people see he is not dead; then we can get this boat turned around, but we may have to hold some of these people up somewhere. Put them in a brig of some sort. Tie them up. They might not come easily. I also want to get into that room and prove what I'm talking about. I'm sure he's been receiving blackmail messages.'

'You're sure?' said Tiff. 'I think I'm the one who's sure about that. We need to get in there, and get the blackmail messages,' said Tiff. 'I think I know who they are coming from, but I'll not say until we get there.'

She was off on her *Miss Marple* effort again. 'It's not a TV show, Tiff. You don't need to leave the drama to the end,' but there was no stopping her. Tiff had made up her mind that she was on top of this case, and she was going to crack it at the right time. Cat breathed deeply. She loved her niece to bits, but seriously, she really needed to get with the idea here. 'Can you help us, Mr Kopeck? Mrs Gosling, can you help us?'

'Okay,' said Sarah. 'How about I pop out, go down the corridor, go up, and see if there's a clear path, and then we can get you up towards Mr Hughes's room, his suite. How are you going to get in?'

'I know the codes,' said Tiff. 'It's not a problem.'

'Good. Well, I'll pop out if Tyrrell stays here with you. Don't come out. It'll be okay. I'll come back when the coast is clear, then he can escort you up just in case something's happening.'

'It's probably better if Mr Kopeck goes,' said Tiff.

'Why?' asked Sarah Gosling.

'Well, as you said, his eyes have been on every other bit of skirt in this place. He'd have a reason to be out and walking about without you. It would be strange for you to be on your own, though. Just a thought.'

'Yes. You're spot-on,' said Tyrrell Kopeck. 'I think I can play that act.'

'You've been playing it all along,' said Sarah. 'The last time I pay money for anybody to come along. Next time I'm going to get a real man. One that wants me.'

Tyrrell Kopeck gave a raise of his eyebrows, but it seemed his heart was in being the actor out on stage, so he turned around, and held his hand up to the three women, 'Stay here. I'll be back shortly. I'll just case the joint.'

As the door closed behind him, Cat shook her head. *Case the joint.* She felt like she was in a TV murder mystery with this man on the go, and it wasn't one she was happy to be in. As she turned around to look at Sarah Gosling, she noted that Tiff was watching her closely. Tiff usually tuned out in such situations. Maybe put her earphones in, eyes miles away, but she was focused on Sarah Gosling as closely as she'd ever seen Tiff focus on anyone.

'I'm sorry about Mr Kopeck, Sarah. It's not easy finding a good man. When you do, you end up losing him.'

'Oh, there's been plenty try to come along now that I've got my millions,' said Sarah. 'Plenty try to hang on, but Tyrrell is not even any fun. You think he could make the effort for the money I'm paying him.'

'What made you think of coming on this anyway,' asked Cat. 'I mean, it seems a little bizarre, although it is a bit more private, but I thought you'd be more of a sunshine person. Go and see the sun.'

'No, I like all this stuff, animals out in the cold sea of the wilds, especially the penguins.'

Cat saw Tiff's eyes raise. 'We haven't seen any up here,' said

Tiff.

'No. It was the other week,' said Sarah a little quickly. 'Before you arrived. Before all this madness started. Even then, Tyrrell was often looking after someone else.'

'Again, I'm sorry,' said Cat. 'But he's useful to us at the moment. At least we know he's not up to any devious ideas. If you can get me to that room and we can find out what's going on, he'd have more than done his work.'

'It's good cover though,' said Sarah. 'Are you sure you trust him? Because I don't trust him in anything. Tyrrell has been swanning about, mixing with any other woman going. It's cover to find out what's happening. He may be in with it.'

'Except that you invited him here,' said Tiff. 'That kind of rules out the premeditated bit.' Cat watched her niece. There was almost a smile coming across her face.

'Well, I don't trust him,' said Sarah Gosling. 'Not one bit.' With that, there was a thump on the door. Entering the room, Tyrrell closed the door behind him and ran his hand through his silver hair. 'There's nobody about. I think the guests are all staying in their quarters,' he said. 'This could be a chance. Who's coming?'

'I think it's best if we all go,' said Tiff. Cat gave her a look. That didn't sound sensible. What if they came round to check the guest quarters and nobody was in? Somebody would need to be in. Even if it's giving cover for everybody else.

'Are you sure, Tiff?' said Cat. 'Not better if one of us stayed behind?'

'Yes,' said Sarah Gosling. 'That would be a good idea.'

Tiff shook her head. Stepping up off the bed, Tiff turned to Sarah Gosling and said, 'I think we're going to need you up there, maybe standing guard outside the door. Nobody will suspect you of anything. You've got no links to this business. The last thing they want to do is have to kill you unnecessarily. All you've got to do is say you were looking for Tyrrell and thought the captain could help.'

'Excellent suggestion,' said Tyrrell. 'Right, ladies, shall we go? I'll pop out the front. Who's going to lead behind me then?'

'I think you should go second,' Tiff said to Cat. 'I'll bring up the rear behind Mrs Gosling.' Catriona sensed something from Tiff. She was in that confident mood, as if she were up on top of the game. Cat wanted to know why. What was that? What was it at this time that made her feel so in charge? But there were too many people here. Not enough time.

Tyrrell stuck his head back out. 'The coast is clear; come on, let's go.' The small party of four crept along the corridor, then up to the next deck and Mr Hughes's cabin. As they stood outside the door, Tiff entered the code, and the door swung open gently. There was no one there. The room was empty, the body bag gone from the bed. Cat held her finger up to her mouth and motioned for Tyrrell to walk in with her.

'You stand outside, nice and quiet,' Tiff said to Sarah. 'If anyone comes, rap the door gently, and we'll get out of here. Don't wait for us. Just disappear.'

Sarah nodded, and Cat watched Tiff smile as she entered the room. Soon, the three of them had searched through the room that Cat had already taken apart. It was just clothes. Nothing but clothing. She went to the other door, ready to have a look at Mr Hughes's private room. Slowly, she pulled the door back and when she saw a pair of feet up on a chair, she stopped moving. Again, she edged the door slightly and heard a snore.

'Looks like the captain's worn him out, Tiff. He's sleeping.'

'Well, then we move quickly,' said Tyrrell. 'We need to find something to tie him with.' The threesome looked at each other, but then the door in front of them swung open. Standing there in the flesh was Ernest Hughes, the supposedly dead millionaire and owner of the vessel. 'How the hell did you get back in here?' he said. Cat's heart skipped a beat, and she moved backwards, but Tyrrell Kopeck simply threw a punch straight to Ernest Hughes's face. It caught him square in the jaw, and the man fell backwards, hitting his head off a table. He lay on the floor.

'Quick,' said Cat, and urged Tyrrell to help pull the man up onto the sofa.

'If Hughes is anything like I've known him,' said Tyrrell Kopeck, 'there'll be plenty of things to tie him up with. I can't believe there was nothing in that room. Check in here.'

'Wait!' said Cat. 'Everybody just go quiet for a minute.' There was nothing. Not a sound. 'Good, now search.' Cat went through a number of drawers in the study room. It had a sofa and a small table, the one that Mr Hughes had cracked his head on. There was also a series of cupboards and drawers along one wall, which Cat was looking into. Tiff was searching in an alcove, while Tyrrell was looking underneath the seats and in the desk drawers of the small study table. Cat pulled open a drawer at the top, and looking in, saw a range of items that she was sure belonged in one of those seedier shops in the side street of some town. However, there were a pair of pink, fluffy handcuffs. Holding them up, she saw Tyrrell Kopeck's face.

'Now that's more like it. I bet there's a load of other things in there.' Cat looked inside. There were, but she certainly wouldn't be trying any of them. She took the handcuffs and went over to the man lying on the sofa. Taking his hands behind his back, she cuffed him and then took a large handkerchief from her niece and put a gag around his mouth. It wasn't perfect, but the man wasn't talking at the moment, anyway, out cold from Tyrrell's punch.

The threesome searched for the next five minutes. With Tyrrell working on the main desk, he found a drawer at the bottom that was locked. Working hard with a knife from amongst some cutlery sitting on the side, he managed to prise the drawer open. Inside was a large brown envelope, which he opened out onto the desk. He looked at a sheet of paper with pieces of newspaper cut out. The words on it were simple. 'You know why. It's not the behaviour of a proper man. Correct this, or else.'

# Chapter 22

‘Well, that's pretty blunt,' said Tyrrell. 'Certainly, no messing about there but it's a bit overdramatic for my liking.'

Cat looked at the man strangely. After all, he was an actor.

'No, seriously, it is a bit overdramatic for me. I'm not that sort of person. I'm quite happy, you know, to push on in this acting business, make a living. Yes, I've pulled a few strings and I've kept quiet about some things that shouldn't really have happened, but that's not me.'

'But it is someone,' said Tiff. 'Someone sent that to him, so he was being blackmailed; that's why you're all here.'

There came a rap on the door. 'No,' said Cat. 'Not now. Quick, Tiff, grab the paperwork. We need to get Mr Hughes out of here.'

'But they are coming in through that door,' said Tyrrell Kopeck, 'And where do we go?'

'He's got to have some access straight out of here,' said Catriona. 'Come on. Can you carry him?'

Tyrrell smiled, 'I'm not a complete has-been. I still have a bit of shape to me.' Cat watched him pick Mr Hughes up, who fortunately was not the tallest man in the world. Tyrrell threw him over his shoulder, and then Cat saw the wince on the man's face. 'It's okay. I'm okay. Let's go, let's go.'

Catriona looked around the room and saw the exit door at the far end. Opening it, she found stairs heading up. Running up them, they came to another opening at the top with a door across it. *This must be near the top of the ship*, thought Catriona, and delicately she opened the door. Looking out, she could see the bridge and the small area behind it which was open deck. *It's going to have to do*, she thought. *We could shout from here, get everybody else up, then they'll see he's alive*. She turned around when she heard the crack of Tyrrell's knee as he climbed the stairs.

'Don't worry. I've had my cod liver oil. It's okay. I'm still going. I'm still going,' he puffed. Beyond him, Cat could see Tiff clutching the ransom note in her hand. Opening the door for Tyrrell, Cat allowed him to carry Hughes out and then set him down in the corner of the open deck. Down below, she could see Tara Limpet and waved at her frantically. Beside her was Harriet Bridge.

On identifying the woman, Cat shouted out loudly, 'Harriet, up here. Now, come up here, now. We found him. We found Mr Hughes. He's alive.'

From beside Harriet Bridge, Demi Forsyth's head appeared and suddenly everyone was coming from everywhere. Cat stood with Tyrrell and Tiff in a small semi-circle around Ernest Hughes while everyone else started to appear on the small, open deck. Pushing through the throng were the forcible shoulders of Captain Jollye.

'What are you doing with that man?' she yelled at them. 'He was inside the bag. The body is kept inside the bag for a reason. You've gone too far this time. Your niece has gone too far.'

'But he's alive,' said Tyrrell. 'I know. I had to knock him out;

he was trying to attack me.'

'And somebody's been trying to blackmail him,' said Tiff, holding up the ransom note. 'That's why you're all here. You're here so you can be spied upon, worked on. Mr Hughes could work out which one of you was blackmailing him, because you all worked for different parts of his companies. You all had dealings with him, and you all knew things about him he didn't want others to know.'

Professor Weber stepped forward. 'I knew it,' he said. 'I knew the man was up to no good. Get him up. Get him up.' Cat turned around with Tyrrell and picked Hughes up by the shoulders and saw his head begin to shake. His hands were tied, and his mouth gagged, but once he was up on his feet, Cat removed the gag, believing the man should have a chance to explain what was going on.

'Out with it,' shouted the professor. 'What's this all about? Why were you faking your own death?'

'I didn't,' said Ernest Hughes, shaking his head groggily. 'Someone tried to kill me. One of you tried to kill me.'

'Oh, yes,' said Heinrich, 'that's likely. Why did you kill Jack Fogherty?'

'I didn't. That was a mistake. That was a terrible mistake, but I didn't kill him.'

'I don't believe you,' said the professor.

'Yes, exactly,' said Harriet. 'How are we meant to believe that? You'd have killed any one of us if you thought we were doing that against you.'

'But it was a mistake.'

'Indeed, it was,' said Tiff, stepping forward, and Cat rolled her eyes. Tiff was about to take the scene, and Cat was panicking. Just what would she come up with?

'Mr Hughes did not order the killing of Jack Fogherty. Jack had his issues. The racing car team he was in, and some methods of coercion that were being used were not appreciated by Jack Fogherty. He was going to bring this to Mr Hughes. I know this because he told me all about cars and his passion for them, and then when we were inside his cabin, we found his diary, and how he found the methods of Mr Hughes repugnant. He was determined to speak to him, and I believe he did speak to him, but he was overheard by someone. Someone working for Mr Hughes. Someone who didn't normally work for him, but was brought in special for a reason.'

'You mean the captain did it? Jollye, you did it.' The professor pointed a finger straight at the woman.

'No,' said Tiff. 'Not the captain. She would die for him, but I'm not sure if she'd murder for him. If she could murder for him, my Aunt would be dead by now. No, this was someone no one suspected because we wouldn't have thought they were in the employ of Mr Hughes. In fact, no one knew they were in the employ of Mr Hughes except for Mr Hughes himself. Isn't that right?'

Cat nearly put her head in her hands. Tiff was standing proudly in front of the crowd, engaging them all and turning around as if she was in the last scene of a murder epic.

'For Pete's sake, Tiff, just tell everybody what's going on. None of the theatrics.' But it fell on deaf ears. As Tiff stepped forward and grabbed Sarah Gosling by the collar. 'This is your killer,' she said.

'Me?' said Sarah Gosling. 'Me? I won a million pounds. I came here for a holiday. I helped you.'

'No. You kept an eye on us. An eye. When you rapped

the door, you made sure we headed up here with a plan to come and solve all this. In fact, you tried to head us off. You were going to come up to the cabin, Mr Hughes's cabin, and there you would have told him exactly what was going on and looked for a way out. Instead, I saw through it. I kept you outside, but you knew he was coming up here and that everybody could follow up and what did we have except that he was being blackmailed? There was no evidence. You and Jack Fogherty, you've made sure of that. The only person that knows you killed Jack Fogherty is Earnest Hughes. You tried to throw the body overboard, but it got caught in the ropes and I realised he'd been tied and bound. It was clumsy, and you were asked to clean up your mess, but you couldn't even do that properly.'

Sarah Gosling grabbed Tiff by the throat, but Tiff merely stepped hard on her foot and Mr Denny, who had been watching, stepped forward with Ivan Popov and grabbed her by the arms.

'Hold her tight,' said Catriona. 'We have emergency services on the way. They'll be here very shortly and they'll sort this out. Until then I'm taking charge of this ship.'

Captain Jollye stepped forward, 'You are not, madam,' she said. 'This is still my ship and I am in charge. I have done nothing wrong.'

'Yes, you have,' said Cat. 'You pretended to cause an explosion. You then hid a man away from us. You've been participating in this whole charade.'

'I told you before, it was not an accident the gun went off. It was an attempt to kill Mr Hughes.'

'No, it wasn't,' said Cat. 'Don't try to spin that one to us.'

Then her niece put her hand on her shoulder, 'I've got it, Cat.

It's okay,' said Tiff. 'Captain Jollye, it's true. Somebody did try to take Earnest Hughes's life. Somebody worked on the gun, caused it to explode. Very clever. You need to be a reasonable professional for that.'

'Reasonable? I am more than reasonable.'

The crowd suddenly parted and stood in the middle holding a gun was Fragrance Paradise. 'I think you'll find that I've always finished my contract whatever.'

'I knew it was you,' said Tiff, 'put up to it by the professor. You're no lover of his. He hasn't got eyes for a girl like you. Too much of a man of the book. All he wants is his statistics and his figures. Not prepared to take chances. Not prepared to play the market properly.'

'I'm not prepared to use banned chemicals in what I make,' said the professor. 'You would taint our institution. You had to be removed. The board wouldn't do it.'

'No, they wouldn't, and yet here I am,' said Hughes, 'but you'll soon be removed.'

Cat stood and looked at the situation. Fragrance Paradise was still holding a flare gun pointed directly at Mr Hughes. Cat was stood off to the side while Tiff was holding the shoulder of Captain Jollye close to the line of fire of Fragrance. Everyone else had peeled away like the Red Sea.

'Enough talk,' said Fragrance. 'If people are coming, I'd better finish the job and then get out of here. I think we've still got our rib on the back, haven't we? It will be enough to get me somewhere. It's up to you if you come along, professor. After all, I still need my money.'

With that, Fragrance stood forward with one foot, raised the flare pistol, and aimed it at Ernest Hughes. As she went to fire, Captain Jollye ran forward screaming. Tiff followed her and then a shot went off. Cat saw the flare ricochet off the shoulder of Captain Jollye. She spun but kept moving forward, grabbing the hair of Fragrance Paradise. Tiff tried to assist but received a sharp blow to the face and fell backwards.

Jollye had her claws on Paradise, and Cat wondered why nobody else moved. Maybe it was the flare pistol that did it, but surely these things only had one shot. Regardless, the two women grappled, and Fragrance and Jollye spun closer to the edge. As they reached the railing, Paradise grabbed her, putting her hand underneath her buttocks, and then spinning on her heel, driving all her force up and underneath the older woman and tossing her clean over the side. But Jollye still had her hands on Paradise, and she swung and hit the side of the ship. The gate at the railing quivered at first, not used to this excessive weight while Fragrance Paradise buckled, her knee hitting the catch. The gate fell open and both women plunged into the sea.

Cat looked around her at a lot of stunned faces who were all simply gawping.

'Mr Denny, get yourself down to the side. Get the lifesaving equipment. Tara Limpet, get into the boat at the back. Bring it round. Mr Popov, take charge here. Keep an eye on Sarah Gosling and make sure Mr Hughes doesn't go anywhere.'

'I will. Where are you going?'

Cat pulled her top off and then removed her trousers. Turning, she shouted to the air, 'To save those idiots.' and ran, jumping through the gap where the gate had been, diving out into the sea. Swimming was one of Cat's joys. Diving was more of a fear, but growing up, she'd been taken every Saturday and taught how to do it. As she hit the water, her hands were in the perfect position. Surfacing, Cat looked around her and saw the flailing arms of Captain Jollye. Fragrance Paradise only a few feet from her and rapidly swimming that direction.

*Oh, heck*, thought Cat, but without hesitation, she began swimming hard towards the pair of women.

They were only one hundred feet away and Cat cut through the water fast, arriving to find Fragrance pushing down on Captain Jollye's head. Cat tried to grab the woman but received a punch to the head in response. Diving, Cat instead attacked the woman's leg, biting her on the thigh. She felt the woman thrash and instantly bit her on the other side as well. As she surfaced, she began to realise she was more at home in the water than the other women.

In the air, she could hear the small boat arriving, Tara Limpet shouting at her. But as the boat pulled up alongside and Tara Limpet reached down to haul Fragrance Paradise out of the water, Cat realised that Captain Jollye was gone.

'She's gone below,' shouted Cat. 'Whatever you do, don't let that woman out of your sight. Hold her down tight.' She saw Tyrrell Kopeck and Demi Forsyth also in the boat, and Cat hoped they were enough to keep Fragrance at bay.

Cat did not have the luxury of seeing how that situation would play out. Captain Jollye had gone underneath and Cat needed to find her. The water was dark, hard to penetrate and see through more than about five or ten meters. But she started swimming around, pushing through the water, looking for anyone, anything. Running out of breath, she surfaced, flicked her head around and realised she was a moderate distance from the boat.

Turning back, she dived again. Working her way through the water, she knew this was a shot in the dark. Jollye could be anywhere in here, and if she couldn't dive deep, Cat would never get her.  But then something caught her eye.  Barely moving in the water, twisting around slowly. She cut through, swimming hard, and then found a hand.  Grabbing it, she pulled herself down the arm attached to it and wrapped her arms around Captain Jollye.

Kicking hard, she pushed for the surface. It seemed like an age before she broke through, but when she did, she gulped in the fresh air. As she laid Jollye back onto her shoulder and put her own body underneath, she waved her hands frantically in the air, hoping that Tara Limpet would see her. When the engine of the boat kicked into life, Cat breathed a sigh of relief. Thirty seconds later, Captain Jollye was being pulled out and onto the boat. When Cat managed to drag herself up with the help of Demi Forsyth, she saw Tara Limpet working hard on the captain. There were a few mouthfuls of air blown into the woman lying on the bottom of the boat, and Demi Forsyth took the helm, driving it back to the main ship.

Once there, Mr Denny assisted Tara Limpet, and took the captain away to a separate room, but by the time she had left, Cat could see she was breathing. She stood there at the back of the boat feeling the cold air around her bare legs, stood in just a t-shirt and pants. She looked out at the water. Twice she'd had to save somebody. Just ironic that the first person she saved put the second one there. On turning around to step back into the boat, she looked up and saw her niece on the top level looking down at her. There was no smile, just a vague thumbs-up, but a friendly hand reached out to her from the lower deck and pulled her up.

'It's good to see you. You survive. Here, I think you need this.' A tumbler was handed to Cat. It was half-full of a colourless, clear liquid. 'Like I said before,' said Ivan Popov, 'you are my kind of woman. I'm much too old, but hey, I can still drink with you.'

'And you can give me a hug as well,' said Cat. 'I'm bloody freezing.'

# Chapter 23

By the time Catriona had got changed, the ship was making its way back towards land. It would take it a good three days to get there, but in the interim, a rescue helicopter had arrived and had taken Fragrance Paradise and Sarah Gosling away. The professor was also taken away as well as the body of Jack Fogherty. There would be plenty of questions once ashore, but Mr Denny had assured the authorities that all those who were dangerous had been taken off the vessel. He had tried to get Mr Hughes to stay, but the authorities had wanted to interview his boss. They said his continued presence on the boat could be dangerous for many people.

Cat realised that Tiff had had a major say in what had gone on. When she saw her lying on the bed after Cat had come out of the shower, there was a grin on the girl's face.

'I told you I knew what was going on. I told you—'

'Stop,' said Catriona, 'Just stop. You stood up there pontificating, going on about things, and you nearly got us killed.'

'No, I didn't.'

'The captain nearly died.'

'That wasn't my fault. She was trying to protect Mr Hughes. At the end of the day, if she really wants to fall in love with somebody like that, that's her own problem.'

Cat shook her head. This was standard for Tiff. Nothing was ever her issue or her fault. Always somebody else's. Always some other reason why it hadn't been due to her.

'By the way, if you'd worked all this out, you could have seen a lot of things a lot earlier. Sarah Gosling, for example.'

'Yes, Sarah Gosling, she was quite clever, wasn't she?' said Tiff, 'but not clever enough to beat me.'

Again, Cat shook her head. 'At least we're safe. We were lucky with the captain, though. She nearly died out there.'

'Yes, I thought you took your time finding her.'

Cat simply looked at her niece. She'd had enough of this and so left the cabin seeking out someone else to talk to. As she made her way out onto the outer deck, she saw Harriet Bridge.

'How are you feeling, Contessa?' she asked. 'That was quite the rescue.'

'Just doing what I had to do. I think the bigger rescue was getting it all sorted before anybody else died.'

'I think you're right. It seemed that some cross-wires were had, but don't underestimate Earnest; he's a brutal man. I've heard rumours of other things he's done, so quite possibly, it could have been on his orders. Sarah Gosling just got the wrong person.'

'Yes, but it was quite an act. Nearly as good as Scott Jones's. I'm glad to see the back of him,' said Cat. 'He took me in.'

'Yes, he took a lot of us in, but I think the real one to feel sorry for here is Louise Jollye. Hughes will probably try to drag her in, get her to take a lot of the flack. If she's any wisdom, she'd get as far away from him as possible.'

'True, if she has any wisdom,' said Cat, looking around and seeing Tyrrell Kopeck approaching. 'If it isn't the great movie star,' said Cat. 'How are you feeling, Mr Kopeck? You were a great help in the end.'

'I'm feeling pretty stupid. Nearly all went wrong, shacking up with a middle-aged lottery winner. It's a good job I didn't fall for her charms.'

'I think she was meant to fall for yours, that was the ploy.'

'I kind of like the TV movies,' he said. 'A lot easier, less of this running around, and my knees are still killing me from lifting him up those stairs.'

Cat laughed, 'Yes, but at least, you're alive. At least, there was no mistake about what you were doing. Yourself and Mrs Bridge were pretty lucky.'

'Indeed,' said Kopeck, 'but I'll need to cut all ties with Mr Hughes. He did help me get to where I am, but after this, there's going to be too much of a stain on him. Doesn't look good in the movie world. Still, I'm sure I'll be able to get hold of something.'

Cat bid the pair farewell and made her way up to the bridge. Chris Denney was steering the ship, and beside him stood Tara Limpet.

'How are you both doing?'

'It's a great day to sail her,' said Chris Denney. 'Never thought I'd be getting the helm like this,' but beside him, Tara Limpet looked a lot sullener.

'It was sad about Jack Fogherty,' said Cat. 'He wasn't the easiest to understand, certainly. Tiff found out. Not that he was interested in Tiff; he seemed interested in you, though.' There were tears in the girl's eyes and she sniffed.

'He just wanted to talk things through with Mr Hughes, that's all. That was the thing about Jack. It's like when he talked about his motor-racing—he just went on and on about it. Delightful in its own way, but when he wanted this corrected, when he wanted this thing changed, he talked and talked about it, too. Of course, his room is right beside Sarah Gosling's. She must have heard and told Mr Hughes. Somehow, she thought she had the order to kill him. I was with him that last night before it happened.'

Tara Limpet turned away and looked out to sea. There were some things that Cat couldn't fix, and this was going to be one of them, but a tap on her shoulder made her smile.

'Up and about and warm again. It's good to see the woman in charge.' Cat turned around to the bald head of Ivan Popov. He looked wrong without a drink in his hand, but he was smiling broadly at her. 'Tonight, I make meal for you and you drink with me. Yes?' he asked.

'Absolutely,' said Cat. 'You and me. I get to put this all behind me, but first I have to go and see someone. I think she'll be struggling.' Ivan Popov nodded, stepped aside to let Cat down the steps that led to the crew quarters. Once there, she rapped on the door of Louise Jollye's cabin.

'Come in,' said a voice. Cat opened the door to see Louise Jollye wrapped up in bed, the duvet around her.

'I hope you don't mind me coming in,' said Cat. 'It's a bit of an awkward situation for you.'

'I didn't know,' said Louise Jollye. 'He was a tough man. When we took you aside, I thought all we were going to do was hold you, keep you to one side until we'd solved who was trying to attack him. I asked him about Jack Fogherty, and he said he must have fallen over. That's when I started clearing everyone, putting them to the rooms. We couldn't have any more accidents. Someone had tried to kill him, and now someone had killed Jack Fogherty. I thought Ernest might be involved, but I didn't know Ernest could kill someone. Now I know what he did and how he hired someone to do it in the form of Sarah Gosling. He's not the man I thought he was. He'll go to jail for this.'

'Maybe he will, maybe he won't,' said Cat. 'Who can tell? Fragrance Paradise attempted to murder you and Mr Hughes, but Hughes's name will be everywhere, and ruined once the press gets the story.'

'Scott knew,' said Louise, 'Scott knew him well. This is my first time, but Scott worked for him before the boat. I think Scott may even have killed for him. I need to get out of here,' she said. 'I need to get away.'

'Then do it,' said Cat. The woman threw back the bedclothes and stood up, wearing a pair of short pyjamas. She came over to Cat, wrapped her arms around her and kissed her gently on the forehead. 'Thank you for saving my life,' she said. 'After all I did to you, you still came.'

'Kind of part and parcel of it all, isn't it?' said Cat. 'I can't let people die, especially someone like you, that could go and be something.' Jollye wrapped her up tight. Cat wondered just how much of a thank you embrace this was and how much was possibly hoping for something else. Cat separated and made for the door.

'It's up to you. Mr Popov is cooking me dinner tonight,' said Cat. 'After that this evening, I thought those of us who remain could all have some cocktails. There's no harm anymore; there's no threat onboard. I think we all need to just chill out until we get to port.'

Louise Jollye nodded, reached back, undid her hair, and let it flop down the side. 'I'll be there,' she said. 'I look forward to it. Maybe you could give me some idea about what I do next.'

Cat nodded and shut the door, and then leant back on it, her eyes rolling to the ceiling. *She wants advice from me*, she thought. *I've ended up on a potentially murderous cruise. At the first chance of getting away from my dead husband's family, I've nearly got myself killed and my niece, and that woman wants advice from me? How bad has it got for her?*

With that, Cat walked back on deck and stared at the surrounding scenery. Soon after, she felt a hand on her shoulder and someone standing beside her.

'Mr Popov said, "Seven o'clock for dinner."'

'Thanks, Tiff,' said Catriona. Before Tiff could walk off, she took her niece by the hand. 'Thank you. You did well—you kept us alive. I think you are the brains of the family.'

'Yes,' said Tiff, as if it was the most obvious thing in the world. 'You didn't do bad for an older woman.' Cat crushed her hands into a fist as her niece walked off. *The cheek of it.* She turned around and walked into Scott Jones, the man who had knocked her out, the man who had zipped her up in a corpse bag, the man who had taken her heart and broken it, the man who should have been a great bit of fun to be away with.

'Contessa, may I apologise and say I'm sorry? I was acting only in the best interest of the ship, and if I may, I would like to accompany you to dinner tonight.'

Catriona almost slumped backwards. *Seriously, did he really think that he had that charm?* With that, she stepped forward and drove her knee up into the man's groin. He doubled over, falling to the floor. 'I'm Contessa Catriona Munroe, and you sir, shall never speak to me again.' With that, Cat strolled off. She may have been in jeans and a T-shirt, but every bit of her felt like Italian royalty.

# Read on to discover the Patrick Smythe series!

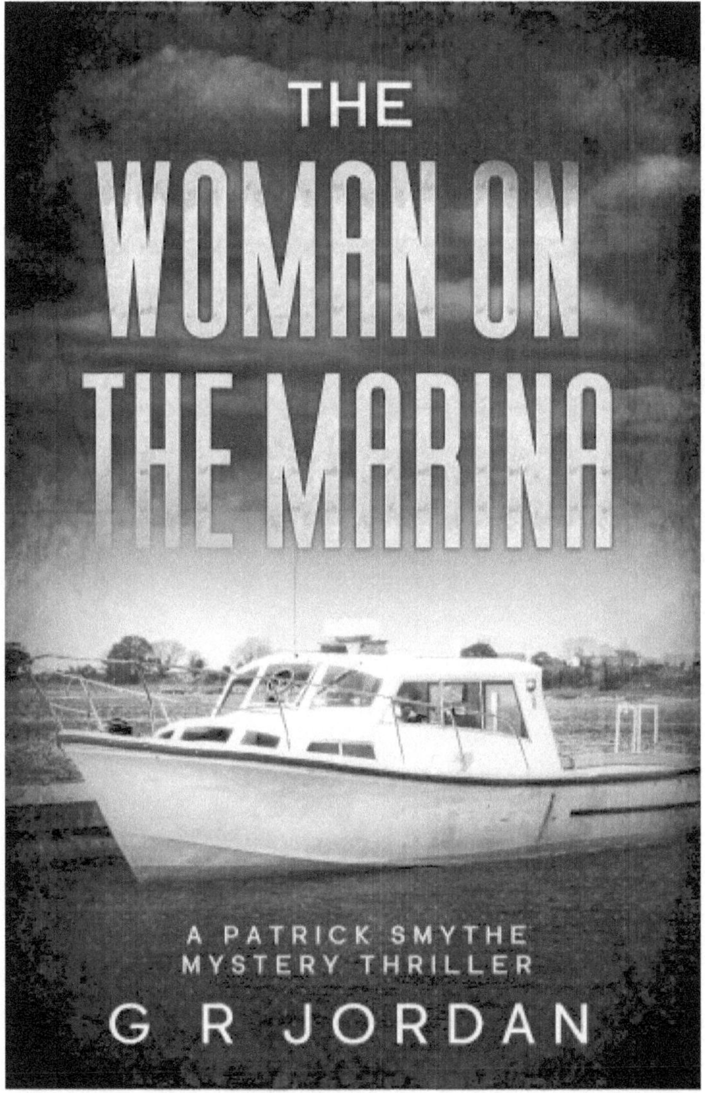


*Start your Patrick Smythe journey here!*

Patrick Smythe is a former Northern Irish policeman who

after suffering an amputation after a bomb blast, takes to the sea between the west coast of Scotland and his homeland to ply his trade as a private investigator. Join Paddy as he tries to work to his own ethics while knowing how to bend the rules he once enforced. Working from his beloved motorboat 'Craigantlet', Paddy decides to rescue a drug mule in this short story from the pen of G R Jordan.

Join G R Jordan's monthly newsletter about forthcoming releases and special writings for his tribe of avid readers and then receive your free Patrick Smythe short story.

Go to https://bit.ly/PatrickSmythe for your Patrick Smythe journey to start!

# About the Author

GR Jordan is a self-published author who finally decided at forty that in order to have an enjoyable lifestyle, his creative beast within would have to be unleashed. His books mirror that conflict in life where acts of decency contend with self-promotion, goodness stares in horror at evil, and kindness blindsides us when we at our worst. Corrupting our world with his parade of wondrous and horrific characters, he highlights everyday tensions with fresh eyes whilst taking his methodical, intelligent mainstays on a roller-coaster ride of dilemmas, all the while suffering the banter of their provocative sidekicks.

A graduate of Loughborough University where he masqueraded as a chemical engineer but ultimately played American football, Gary had worked at changing the shape of cereal flakes and pulled a pallet truck for a living. Watching vegetables freeze at -40'C was another career highlight and he was also one of the Scottish Highlands "blind" air traffic controllers.

These days he has graduated to answering a telephone to people in trouble before telephoning other people to sort it out.

Having flirted with most places in the UK, he is now based in the Isle of Lewis in Scotland where his free time is spent between raising a young family with his wife, writing, figuring out how to work a loom and caring for a small flock of chickens. Luckily, his writing is influenced by his varied work and life experience as the chickens have not been the poetical inspiration he had hoped for!

**You can connect with me on:**

🌐 https://grjordan.com

📘 https://facebook.com/carpetlessleprechaun

**Subscribe to my newsletter:**

✉ https://bit.ly/PatrickSmythe

# Also by G R Jordan

G R Jordan writes across multiple genres including crime, dark and action adventure fantasy, feel good fantasy, mystery thriller and horror fantasy. Below is a selection of his work. Whilst all books are available across online stores, signed copies are available at his personal shop.

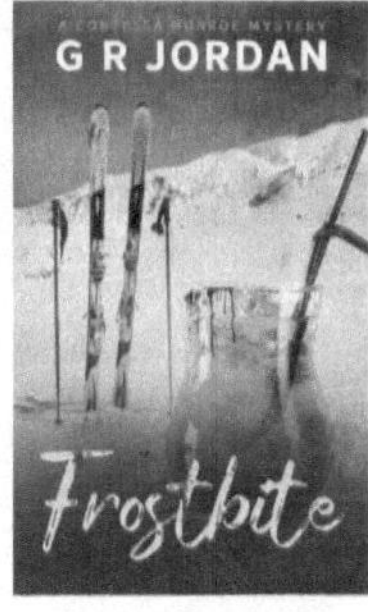

**Frostbite: A Contessa Munroe Mystery #2**
**An elite ski resort suffers a power failure threatening the safety of its guests. As the residents run supplies between the stricken lodges, a body is found butchered in the snow. Can the Contessa and Tiff discover who likes to truly carve up on the ice?**

A fortnight of indulgence turns into two weeks of survival as an avalanche and stormy conditions cut off the exclusive Monte Rosa resort. But as the cold sets in with the power lines down, the Contessa finds out there are more deadly things on the slopes than snow and ice.

Watch your back when they only ski on the red slopes!

**The Satchel (Highlands & Islands Detective Book 11)**

https://grjordan.com/product/the-satchel

**A bag is found hanging on a lonely tree in an Inverness park. Inside, a morbid collection of fists tell a tale of murder and intrigue. Can Macleod find the killer and stop a second show of hands?**

Battle-weary Macleod must seek to understand a murderer's obsession when a bag of appendages turns up in a local park. But as the links between the victims become more apparent, the possible identities of the killer increases. Can Macleod sift the wheat from the chaff and stop the killer before another bag is full?

Don't raise your hand if you know what's good for you!

**Highlands and Islands Detective Thriller Series**
https://grjordan.com/product/waters-edge
Join stalwart DI Macleod and his burgeoning new DC McGrath as they look into the darker side of the stunningly scenic and wilder parts of the north of Scotland. From the Black Isle to Lewis, from Mull to Harris and across to the small Isles, the Uists and Barra, this mismatched pairing follow murders, thieves and vengeful victims in an effort to restore tranquillity to the remoter parts of the land.

Be part of this tale of a surprise partnership amidst the foulest deeds and darkest souls who stalk this peaceful and most beautiful of lands, and you'll never see the Highlands the same way again

**The Disappearance of Russell Hadleigh (Patrick Smythe Book 1)**
https://grjordan.com/product/the-disappearance-of-russell-hadleigh
**A retired judge fails to meet his golf partner. His wife calls for help while running a fantasy play ring. When Russians start co-opting into a fairly-traded clothing brand, can Paddy untangle the strands before the bodies start littering the golf course?**

In his first full novel, Patrick Smythe, the single-armed former policeman, must infiltrate the golfing social scene to discover the fate of his client's husband. Assisted by a young starlet of the greens, Paddy tries to understand just who bears a grudge and who likes to play in the rough, culminating in a high stakes showdown where lives are hanging by the reaction of a moment. If you love pacey action, suspicious motives and devious characters, then Paddy Smythe operates amongst your kind of people.

Love is a matter of taste but money always demands more of its suitor.

**Surface Tensions (Island Adventures Book 1)**

https://grjordan.com/product/surface-tensions

**Mermaids sighted near a Scottish island. A town exploding in anger and distrust. And Donald's got to get the sexiest fish in town, back in the water.**

"Surface Tensions" is the first story in a series of Island adventures from the pen of G R Jordan. If you love comic moments, cosy adventures and light fantasy action, then you'll love these tales with a twist. Get the book that amazon readers said, "perfectly captures life in the Scottish Hebrides" and that explores "human nature at its best and worst".

Something's stirring the water!